FUTILE FLAME

Book 2 of the Vampire Gene

Also by Sam Stone

KILLING KISS

To Kerry,

FUTILE
FLAME

Book 2 of the Vampire Gene

SAM STONE

love Sam Stone x x x

First Edition
- 2009 -

First published in Great Britain by
The House of Murky Depths, 2009.

ISBN: 978-1-906584-08-5

www.murkydepths.com
www.murkydepths.net

Cover concept, design and layout: Martin Deep
Special thanks to editors:
Anne Stringer and Vicky Charville

Printed in the UK by
The Good News Press Limited
Ongar, Essex

Dedication

For David.
For your love, support and encouragement, without which this
book may never have seen the light of day. I love you.

With thanks to my editor Terry Martin

Special thoughts and best wishes to my friend Tanith Lee

Present

Cry.

It won't make any difference. Once we have set our minds to possess your blood then nothing will save you. Though mostly we are merciful and only take what we need, sometimes we need to kill. Lilly has taught me, in her simple fashion, what it is to be truly immortal. We are above the law. Fear of the future, fear of mankind, is a form of self-delusion I have held for centuries. Immortals cannot be killed by man. But now I am sounding somewhat biblical. Forgive me. Quoting from the past is such a part of my nature.

Plead.

The woman won't stand a chance. Her mousey hair, plain face, dowdy clothes and downcast eyes are all part of the attraction. She is older than she seems, almost forty and still single. Our victim is a real 'nobody'. Already I have plucked from her mind the lack of family interest in her life. She will not be missed. She is called Ellie and works for the local church. I am reminded of the Beatles song. There is an irony in the similarity and the chances of us finding our own Eleanor Rigby. It makes her all the more appealing.

I am Gabriele Caccini, Italian by birth and vampire by nature. I am over four hundred years old. And Lilly, she is my love and my only successful re-born mate in all that time. All my other loves died on the night I loved them, the night I took their blood to sate my own hunger.

I look to Lilly as she licks her lips. She has decided; tonight we will kill. Lilly's teeth grow over her lip as we follow Ellie through the streets towards her empty, lonely flat. Ellie hitches her rucksack up onto her shoulder and hurries along past a noisy bar as four drunken men tumble out. They don't notice her: she almost has a talent for invisibility as she scurries up the street. She stops hesitantly in a graffiti-covered doorway and searches her pocket for keys. This unobtrusive entrance marks her home. A spider spins a web in one corner and I notice that the paint is peeling from the door. She lives above a shop. It's called Booze Snooze. It's a bargain drinks store and attracts all kinds of unsavoury characters. The doorway to her flat is dark and hidden. It is full of shadows. Good. Even the access aids us.

We sweep forward in a cloud of invisibility, but some sixth sense makes Ellie glance frantically over her shoulder. Her eyes are a non-descript brown. She cannot see us, but anxiety makes her heart leap as she feels a stir in the atmosphere.

Death is coming, Ellie.

I can see the terror flicker in her eyes. It's as though she is aware of us as she peers into the dark in our direction. We stand across the road, waiting for her to open her door.

The streets are busy, too many people passing, a stream of traffic: all of this could make our sport more risky but it only adds to the excitement. I feel aroused as I take Lilly's hand in mine, rubbing my thumb against her palm. She shudders. I feel her sexual energy surge through my fingers.

'I want her,' she murmurs.

I chuckle quietly in my throat. 'Wanting' has so little to do with sex for us and everything to do with need.

'Whatever Lilly wants, Lilly gets,' I whisper, kissing her neck.

She curls into my arms. Her anticipation ripples around me. I kiss her passionately and then we turn, still embracing. We watch Ellie like voyeurs, our heads pressed together, as she fumbles with the lock in her front door. It creaks and groans. It needs oiling. Her aura is a mass of memories and thoughts, mostly mundane. Ellie's life has been one of drudgery. She has never experienced luxury, has never felt her life had any meaning. She has barely noticed the years pass by because she has been so focused on surviving the daily hardships and on worshipping a God who does not know she exists. Now, at least, something different is happening in her world and her ending will have some significance. There is poetry in death. Mortals don't know it. Sometimes it's beautiful. Other times, sickening. Violent death leaves an imprint on society. Ellie's end may even be reported, giving her some form of immortality even though her life has added nothing to the world.

Blood oozes from my lip as I bite down in subconscious response. I am imagining her taste. Will her blood be bitter? Or merely tired? Blood itself has an essence of the person's life. It tells a story. I have hundreds of them. The memories of a life taken remain in my subconscious to be recalled at will. I suspect, though, that Ellie's will not be so memorable.

A double-decker bus turns the corner and drives slowly down the street towards us. I watch it with curiosity as it slows and comes to a stop, blocking our view of Ellie's doorway. A tall skinny boy in a hooded top jumps off the bus, avoiding the steps and narrowly missing us as we step back in a reflex to prevent a collision. The boy shudders as his body touches our invisible auras, and he pulls his hood further around his ears as he walks down the street towards the pubs and the nightlife. The bus moves away.

Ellie is gone.

I look up at the flat and wait for the telltale lights to switch on but nothing happens.

'Where did she . . ?' Lilly asks, drawing away from me.

'She must have changed her mind and gone somewhere else. Perhaps she couldn't open the door.' I scan the area for a trace of her aura. 'This way.'

We run down the street in the direction from which the bus came. Lilly tugs at my hand. She is hungry. We haven't fed for two weeks. We pick up Ellie's scent a few blocks away. Lilly rushes headlong into a narrow side street then stops.

'She was here. But now ...'

'Gone. Again.'

We stare at each other, confused. Then I turn and look down the street, examining every house. It is a tapered terraced row with tiny front gardens that are made of concrete. Maybe she is visiting one of the occupants. A dull light throws shadows on the cream coloured blinds of the first house. Further down I see a woman yanking the curtains closed over an upstairs bedroom window. There is nothing extraordinary about this road. Ellie's essence is here but she isn't, and I can't sense her in any of the houses.

Darkness.

I feel a change in the air. I look up. There is a hollow patch in the sky and I experience a moment of disorientation. Something is falling. It seems like a black hole has disengaged itself from the rest of the heavens. It gathers momentum and I'm frozen, fascinated, as I watch it fall towards me.

Lilly gasps, grabs my arm and pulls me away as something thumps to the ground at my feet, precisely where I'd been standing. The noise of breaking bones and punctured organs deafens my mind.

'Oh my God.'

Lilly bends to examine the body. It is Ellie. Her face is smashed but the smell of her blood is unmistakable. Her throat has been mauled as if an animal has attacked her, but we know different.

'Vampire,' Lilly whispers, confirming my thoughts. 'But why steal her from us?'

I shake my head. The only other vampire I know is Lucrezia and this is not her handiwork. I bend down. There is a thick black substance oozing from the gaping wound on Ellie's neck. It is not blood. Lilly reaches out to touch it.

'Don't,' I hiss, grabbing her hand.

'What is it?'

'I don't know, but it looks unhealthy.'

There is a wailing screech and we both look up as something

leaps from wall to wall down the street. It is fast, agile and leaves an aura unlike any I have ever seen before. With a final triumphant cry, it soars up onto one of the rooftops and away.

Lilly and I look at each other in silence.

'What was that thing?' she asks, but I can't answer.

It felt old. It smelt – unique. It oozed power. This creature is certainly an immortal. Vampiric in nature, though very different from us. For the first time in four hundred years I actually feel vulnerable. I have to find out who or what this entity, this creature, is and I know just the person to speak to.

Chapter 1 - Present

Mortuary

'I suppose it is pointless to ask how you found me,' Lucrezia says through her mask, raising her blood-covered hand as though in greeting.

I sit down slowly on a wooden chair in the corner of the mortuary, well back from the gruesome spectacle of the female corpse she is dissecting. I can see her face framed by the cadaver's blood and mud-caked feet.

This cold, stark, white-painted room with its clinical cleanliness is the last place I would have expected such a vivacious creature to be working. But then, Lucrezia is always full of surprises.

'When I want to find you, I can.' I remain still, concerned that I might spook her.

She is a magnet drawing me ever closer to her, despite my beautiful Lilly who keeps my feet firmly on the ground with her twenty-first-century-girl common sense.

'And I, you.'

I let this little piece of information sink in. So, she can always find me. Does she know then? Does she care that I have added to our numbers? Is Lilly in danger? Panic surges forward but I quickly quell the sensation; animals can sense fear and so can vampires.

'I mean you no harm,' I say calmly, hoping she feels the same, although going up against each other would be an interesting prospect, one I've often wondered about. Can one immortal kill another?

Lucrezia puts down the large scalpel she was using as I entered. She gazes down at the 'Y' shaped incision, which curves from the shoulders, under the girl's breasts and joins at the sternum. The line traces down as far as her pubis, leaving a faint red stain on the blue white skin.

Lucrezia removes the blue theatre mask from her face and looks at me over the rim of her glasses. The glass in them is clear, not prescription because her eyesight is perfect. Does she wear them as a disguise or because she thinks they make her look more intellectual? She turns away, reaches behind her to an instrument trolley and lifts a small saw with a round head; it springs to life in her hands, purring like a cat being caressed by a loving owner.

'Do you know what this is, Gabriele?'

I don't answer.

'It's a bone saw. I use it to cut through the breast bone and the skull of a corpse in order to determine the cause of death.'

Lucrezia demonstrates. She reaches down and roughly scrapes back the skin from the girl's chest, exposing the ribs beneath. The saw bites into the bare bone of the dead girl as she lies on the stainless steel slab. Minute particles of bone dust and traces of blood spin off into the air and splash briefly onto Lucrezia's clean blue theatre robes and across the lenses of her glasses but she presses harder until a loud crack echoes in the room. The saw's purring changes pitch. Like the song of a Siren, it is hopelessly hypnotic, powerfully beautiful. Hideous. But all too brief. The silence is deafening as she turns the instrument off.

Her gloved hands reach down, fingers pressing along the edges of the cut bone until they find their grip. The wound yawns as she pulls the two halves apart with a practised shrug.

'Are you trying to psyche me out?' I smile.

There is no horror in the dead for me, not since I spent several nights locked in a cabin of the *Princess Marie* with my dead wife Amanda. I had watched her corpse rot, denying that I had killed her as she failed to rise. So, no, Lucrezia's behaviour is far from intimidating.

'Why? Is it working?'

'No. It reminds me of a movie I saw once – *Re-Animator*. A cheap, nasty, slash-horror. Not frightening, but rather silly.'

She stops, her hand still inside the chest cavity.

'Mmmm. So you think I'm rather silly? Well actually it might surprise you to know: I'm just working; certainly not trying to gross you out, Gabriele.'

I stand slowly as she lifts the heart from the girl's chest with infinite care. She places the still, diseased organ onto a weighing scale that hangs beside the autopsy table. She looks at the LCD below briefly before turning to the unit behind her, where a computer with a flat screen monitor and a plastic covered keyboard waits. She taps quickly on the keyboard and the weight of the heart registers on the monitor.

'What do you want?'

As she speaks, she removes her soiled gloves and throws them casually onto the bare stomach of the corpse.

'You know I look you up from time to time. Sometimes you've made sure I saw you. Like the last time – your club in New York.'

It was the perfect hunting ground for a vampire and I understood why she would want to be there. But instead of her usual indifference she had warned me of the forthcoming AIDS epidemic. Then, she had tried to seduce me.

'That's ancient history. I only do real work now.'

'Why?'

Lucrezia raises an eyebrow and looks at me; she seems surprised by the question. She stares at me for a moment as if considering her answer. Perhaps she is unsure herself why she 'works'.

'I want to be useful. I want to learn new things.'

'And this coming from a woman who only wanted to experience new male lovers,' I laugh. 'What's really in it for you? Because you know I don't believe that.'

'That's a bit of an assumption. Who said all of my lovers were male?'

Lucrezia strips off her scrubs, stuffing them into a basket under the cabinet, to reveal blue jeans and a tee-shirt. She removes the glasses, placing them beside the computer. She is beautiful: blonde natural curls, tied back into a neat ponytail with pale green eyes and a slender, but curvaceous frame. She looks like a young woman, barely old enough to be an intern, but I know better. She was born in 1480 and did not die in 1519 regardless of the historical records that say she did. But she looks to all intents and purposes like a modern girl. Even I have difficulty remembering that she is a monster when she looks at me through such youthful features.

'I do not waste my immortality, Gabriele. Unlike you with your playboy lifestyle. I use my accumulated knowledge to inform my work.'

She stands with her hand on her hip. She is young, stunning and I burst out laughing.

'What is so amusing?'

'Well ... I just don't know how you get away with it. Looking like you do.'

Her eyes narrow slightly and for a moment I see her age and experience reflected in her black pupils as rage surges into them in a visible rush. She straightens her spine, losing the sloppy modern stance she's adopted and her old arrogance reappears in the straight line of her shoulders. She, like me, has always been an excellent mimic.

'At least that posture is more like the real you.'

'What would you know?' She folds her arms over her chest. 'What are you really doing here, Gabriele? Because I know it is not that you felt like looking me up.'

I imitate her posture before I realise I'm doing it. We are two old enemies unsure if the feud still remains.

I force my arms down by my side, trying to remain still for fear that she will think I'm defensive. After all, I need her knowledge, despite my ridicule of it. I need to know more of her past. Because then maybe I can understand how my only success, after years of trying to make a mate, was Lilly – a direct descendant of my own daughter, Marguerite. More than ever I need to know if there is any threat to our continued existence. The entity we encountered in Turin and later in England has left me with an uneasiness that I cannot shake. I'm afraid for Lilly more than myself. But how then can I persuade Lucrezia to tell me about her life without revealing too much about mine?

'Something has happened.'

'Really? And I'm interested because?'

'It may affect you.'

'You've told someone, haven't you? You've fallen for some little tart who'll die once you fuck and feed, because everyone knows that's how you get off, and then ...'

'Whoa ... How would you know how I "get off", Lucrezia? You, who only have one-night stands. I've built relationships, loved even, while you isolate yourself by working in a mortuary. What's that, some morbid obsession with death? Or maybe there's something more to it?'

She is silent, face blank, and I begin to regret my outburst as she slowly turns to the body of the dead girl. I find myself wondering who she is, how she died. I scrutinise her face and, as if she understands my interest in the girl, Lucrezia explains.

'Poor kid. Only twenty-two. Major heart failure after using "E" for the first time. Seen the state of the heart? Looks like one of our lot sucked it dry,' Lucrezia tells me as she picks up the heart and places it back inside the dead girl's chest.

'How do you know it was drugs?' I ask despite myself.

'Experience. Plus I can smell it on her. Here,' she beckons me forward with her now blood stained fingers. 'Breathe in. Can you smell that?'

'Yes. Sickly sweet. But subtle.'

'Exactly. A tantalising smell. Prolonged abuse would give her organs the odour of Royal Jelly. So, clearly a first timer. Of course, I have to back myself up with medical evidence which means blood analysis and pathology on the remains.'

I am bewildered by her. How does this lovely creature ever understand this? Why would she want to? But I daren't ask her these questions. It seems too intrusive. Though, more than anything, I fear her scorn at my ignorance.

'But look at the state she's in.' She points to the cuts and abrasions on her legs, the filth-covered feet. 'Her friends gave her the drug, but didn't look after her. She was found dead in a ditch.'

Put that way I imagine the grief of the girl's family. And I'm beginning to understand a little why Lucrezia is here.

'So. Tell me. What have you done that may affect me?' She asks quickly changing the mood.

Turning to the sink behind her she begins to scrub the blood from her fingers. I watch with hypnotic fascination. She is meticulous as she cleans her short nails. Once done she tears a strip of blue paper towel from the dispenser above the sink and dries her hands before turning back to the body.

She pushes the corpse away from her work area towards a wall lined with doors and presses a pedal on the trolley to lower it to floor level. As she opens one of the bottom doors, cold air rushes out of the fridge sending wisps of freezing condensation into the atmosphere. The wheels beneath it collapse under as she presses the trolley into the opening, pushing hard against the lip of the doorframe. The remains slide into the coffin-like space and the door clicks shut, swallowing it like the mouth of some tiny frozen hell.

I tear my gaze away from the polished steel to find Lucrezia once more washing her hands at the sink in the far corner of the room. I know I have to tell her, but where to begin?

'My shift is over,' she says. 'Let's go talk.'

'Thank you.'

She stares at me, her eyes round. 'Why are you thanking me?'

'For allowing me your time.'

'Perhaps I should have done that sooner.'

Suburban Vampire

I leave my hired car in the hospital car park and climb into Lucrezia's battered BMW. She is clearly not going for ostentation these days. I want to know why, because I am sure that she, like me, has accumulated much wealth over the years, and money ensures we are always able to hide among the living without fear. Yet here she chooses to live simply. Maybe this is a game for her, like my frequent trips into the 'real world' have been. Pretending to be something I am not has always been part of the fun, but not anymore: Lilly has changed everything for me.

But then, Lucrezia has dabbled in medicine for several years now. In the 1980's, when I met her in a New York club, she told me she was a haematologist. She'd warned me of the coming AIDS epidemic and the effect it would have on my blood if I drank from an infected victim. However, since my main interest was in virgins, it was hardly likely that I would contract the Human Immunodeficiency virus. Even so, her warning had gone a long way to reinforce my choice of victim, and to ensure that I always checked my food carefully before biting into it.

We drive out of the hospital grounds and turn swiftly onto the main road heading towards the motorway. Lucrezia presses down hard on the accelerator with the recklessness of an immortal. We are so secure with our infinity, that speeding never holds any fear for us, so I relax in the seat beside her. On the dash is a security pass. It reads *Dr Lucy Collins* alongside a photograph of Lucrezia.

'Where are we going?' I ask.

'Not far.'

We drive two short miles down the motorway and come off at the first exit. I settle down and close my eyes. There is no need to look; I can always find my way here again if I wish. Lucrezia's aura is radar and always has been. We travel for around twenty minutes, weaving in and out of streets with short bursts of motorway in between.

We arrive sooner than I expect. I open my eyes as Lucrezia parks the car smoothly on the drive of a suburban house with a dark blue painted front. I scrutinise it with interest. I know that she could have any house in any place; yet, she is in Manchester, the place I first met Lilly. It looks like the sort of house a doctor would have. I almost expect a husband and children waiting behind the double-glazed front door. But as we climb from the car, I know that her life will be absent of companionship of any kind.

She unlocks the door with a key ring, which also sports a tacky disc with a faded picture of the Statue of Liberty on it. It reads 'so good they named it twice' in bold red letters. Can it be that she is sentimental about her previous lives?

The door opens without a sinister creak, so there is nothing predictable or corny about this vampire's residence. As we enter the hallway, which is quite long with a staircase to the left, I'm shocked by the magnolia blandness of the décor. It lacks imagination – though it looks clean.

There are some Art Deco influences present. Black curved chandeliers hang from the ceiling, but the whole effect is minimalist right down to the taupe pattern-less carpet. This is a far cry from the life I live with Lilly.

'Can I get you anything?' Lucrezia asks.

The normality of her home, her manners, are so strange to me, that I experience a slight sense of unreality. I realise then that I am in shock: stunned by her nearness and this sudden change in her attitude and lifestyle.

'Am I supposed to reply, "Yes please, a coffee would be good"?'

'If you want coffee, I can get it for you.'

'No. I don't need anything.'

She leads me into the lounge, a smallish room, sparse, with an uncomfortable upright three-piece suite of brown leather on a cream carpet. I fight back a snigger. Clearly she's trying too hard to appear bland.

'So, what do you want to know?' she asks.

I tear my eyes from the pale blown vinyl paper. For a minute I can't focus on her words, can't remember why I'm here.

'How did all this happen?' I say, although it is as if I am merely asking a mundane question, like, 'How are you?'

'Ah.'

She falls silent and I wait, patience always my virtue.

'I have an uncharacteristic urge to ... talk.' She crumples onto one of the sofas.

'I'm listening.'

'There are things that happened, things I haven't thought of for years. Perhaps, never wanted to think about. And certainly never wanted to speak of.'

Her hands cover her face, then swoop up into her hair, making her appearance manic and almost desperate as she tugs briefly at her blonde locks.

'What is it specifically that you need to know?' she asks.

'I'm not sure. Could you start at the beginning?'

'No. That's too ... raw, although I'm sure that sounds insane to you.'

'No, it doesn't. I understand that feeling perfectly.'

She falls silent again, sitting with her knees pulled up to her chest, her thumbnail pressed between her teeth. She looks like a small and frightened child and my heart opens to her in a way I'd never expected. I feel an affinity and I am on the cusp of learning why.

'I'll start with Caesare.'

'Your brother?'

'Someone did their homework!'

'Lucrezia, your entire family history is in public libraries all over the world. I obviously came across them at some point.'

Her eyes pierce my casual words with disbelief.

'Ok. I looked you up. They made a television series about you and your family – maybe you saw it?'

'I don't watch television.'

'Probably just as well – they didn't make any of you look good.' I realise my mistake as she frowns.

'Don't let's be distracted. You were saying?' I say quickly.

'I think I'll start in the middle,' she decides and then changes her mind. 'No, I won't. It has to begin in the library at St Peter's.'

'Is this the beginning, then?'

'Yes.'

Typical woman, contrary even in immortality! How alike she and Lilly are.

Chapter 3 - Lucrezia's Story

Seducer

'Luci. Where are you going in such a hurry?'

I stopped in the corridor and turned to find my brother Caesare leaning in the open doorway to the library.

'Have you seen Father?'

'No.'

I looked closely at Caesare; his eyes looked strange, as though he had the beginnings of a fever.

'Come in here a moment.'

'Oh Caesare. I'm in no mood for your teasing today. I need to see Father!'

'Come,' he smiled. 'I have something to show you.'

'Alright, but only for a moment. I really do need to ...'

I entered the library, lifting up my pale blue skirt as I stepped over the threshold.

I had searched the halls of the Vatican for my Father; walked down the huge corridor, its many doors beckoning me in, but all barred from me by politics. By then Father was known as Pope Alexander VI, but his birth name was Borgia, and he ruled Rome as though he were a modern Caesar, all in the name of God. But to us he was still Father, and our family lived in the *Palazzo* Maria del Portico, which was attached to St Peter's. We had our own private door to walk in and out of the Vatican whenever we wished and more importantly, Father could visit his mistress Guila Farnese. In those days a Pope could have lovers, though discretion was still important. Father was powerful. No one questioned him. And those that dared risked their lives and those of their entire family.

That morning I needed to see him urgently. He had announced the night before that I was to be married. At first the announcement did not concern me; Father had already made two previous matches. He did this to gain political advantage, not that I understood this. Even so, I always felt safe in the knowledge that he would change his mind again as politics dictated. However, his inclusion of a wedding date troubled me. He'd never allowed things to go that far before. As with the previous arrangements I had not met my fiancé. Father kept me safely away from contact with any men and I was always chaperoned in public.

The Vatican library was very impressive. I rarely visited it in those days, but was always pleased by the high and ornately decorated ceilings. The walls were covered with beautiful leather -bound books of all kinds. I'd often wanted to wander among them but was rarely allowed. And I loved the shape of the room which was curved and seemed to frame the broad desk that stood in the middle. Two tapestry-covered sofas stood either side of a large, white marble fireplace, a comforting feature. And before the fire was an exquisite Persian rug, thick and plush with stunning and vibrant coloured patterns, depicting hunting warriors and square figures, feeding square animals.

'So, why do you need Father in such a hurry?' Behind me Caesare closed the door.

'The marriage. I'm concerned.'

'Ah. I am also,' he replied, walking past me to the desk.

'You are?'

I studied his broad shoulders as he moved back to Father's desk. I wondered whether he was merely teasing me again. He had never appeared to take the slightest interest in Father's dealings with me, other than maybe to agree with his comments. For a long time Caesare stood by the desk gazing down at an open book with barely any acknowledgement that I was there. I watched his expression. My brother was an attractive man. His features were elegant and his long pale blond hair, the same colour as mine, was tied back with a leather thong at the nape of his neck. I had given him that thong myself for his 16th birthday and was pleased to see he still wore it. He was dressed elegantly as always in black breeches and velvet cream coloured surcoat. He was tall, and unlike Father, he was slender. The long fingers of one hand rested on the desk beside the book as he gazed down intently at the page, while his other hand stroked the colourful image. I was intrigued. He seemed mesmerised. I could vaguely make out patterns and shapes on the page from my position near the main door. I took a step towards him then halted, feeling strangely uncomfortable about intruding.

'What do you want to show me?' Apprehension caused the hairs to stand up on my arms and neck as he turned his attention back towards me.

His eyes were strange. Heated in a way I couldn't understand. They shone with a mysterious excitement. He walked towards me, stopped, looked into my eyes and I quickly looked down. They were too intense. Then he walked around me and turned the lock in the library door. I shivered.

'This,' his voice was cheerful, but forced.

He took my hand and led me back towards the study desk. Here lay a vast and exquisite book. It was open somewhere in the middle and even close up I still could not make sense of the images until Caesare twisted it around to face me, waving me forward, so that I could see the picture he had been looking at. The illustration was beautiful. A man and woman, embracing. Exotic colourful clothing dripped from the top half of their bodies. The woman's legs were wrapped around the man as he kneeled between her thighs. Her breasts were bare. I gasped.

'What is it?' I asked.

Excitement mingled with shock as I involuntarily stepped forward.

'It's a very special book. One that Father paid a small fortune for.'

'They are half naked.'

'Yes.'

I found myself drawn to the image. Scrutinized it carefully, observed the stiff rod that protruded from the man and seemed to pierce the woman.

'Is he hurting her?'

'No. It's pleasurable.'

'Oh.'

I was fifteen. Caesare lifted my skirt.

'Let me show you. There's a small space, here ...' His voice, matter of fact, implied knowledge of things that I should know, things I had suspected but was unsure of.

His fingers fumbled inside my underwear, pulled them down around my knees as his hand deftly pushed between my legs, making me open a little as he kneeled down at my feet. I stumbled, hand resting on his shoulder to stop myself falling. His touch made me afraid though I didn't understand why.

'What are you ... ? I don't think you should do that, Caesare.'

'Haven't you ever noticed this? Right here?'

My knees went weak.

'Oh.'

'See. It's nice isn't it? Now, just let me ...'

Half pain, half pleasure paralysed me then.

'Don't,' I gasped.

All the time I wanted to demand he stop, but could not force the words from my lips as his finger continued to induce a pulsing warmth inside me that made me feel wet and hot.

'Yes. You like it don't you?' His voice sounded thick and husky.

I shuddered and trembled against him. Wanting him to stop but hoping he wouldn't, until this mystery was complete, this pleasure fulfilled. A wave curled up from my loins, stretching out, spreading through my small breasts as I fell onto his hand, spasms clenching inside me and my first orgasm poured over his fingers. My knees gave out. Caesare caught me and lay me beneath him, withdrawing his hand as the last pulses rocked through my body.

'Oh. Luci ...' he moaned, pressing his lower body against mine.

He pushed my legs apart as he fumbled with his breeches. I felt insensible. Lay helpless beneath him. And only when I felt him press hard against me did I react and pull away.

'What are you doing?'

'Giving you some more pleasure.'

'No, Caesare. Stop it! It hurts. Don't.'

His lips pressed down on mine, silencing me as he positioned himself more securely between my thighs. I felt trapped, unable to move as he held my flailing arms down above my head. For a moment he held my hands one handed as he reached down, but it wasn't his fingers I felt this time. I squirmed, trying to break free, twisting my head away from his lips.

'Caesare, Stop it!'

But then it was too late as he ground his pelvis into mine and an agonising pain shot through my loins. I felt something rip. I thought he was tearing me up inside. I tried to scream but his lips found mine again, forcing them apart and my cries were muffled and lost inside his mouth. I struggled against him, biting his lip until he yelped and cuffed me against the side of my head. I was numbed, shocked into stillness. The pain in my head and body receded until I lay like a broken doll beneath him. His heavy breath matched his pace. And I lay, dazed, afraid and unable to fight as I was raped and corrupted in the library of St Peter's. The agonising pain left me numb and cold as my virgin blood leaked onto the back of my skirt.

When he cried my name against my bruised lips I knew I could never tell anyone that my brother had defiled me. It was my fault. I let him touch me. I let him give me pleasure. I'd willingly looked at Father's book, even though I'd realised immediately that it was corrupt. I'd encouraged him. He was a man and I'd been warned of male lust.

'Luci.'

I didn't move.

'Luci. Get up. Straighten your clothes and then go back to the house and clean yourself.' Caesare kneeled above me, worry furrowing his brow as he stared into my dulled eyes.

'Caesare ...'

'Come on. Before Father returns.'

'I wanted to see Father.'

'Yes. I know. But not now, not like this.'

I let him pull me to my feet. I caught sight of my dishevelled state in the mirror across the wall behind the desk. My previously coiffured hair was tumbling down at the back and my lips were red and swollen from the way my brother had kissed me. My clothing was creased. It was all evidence that I was shameless, a whore.

I picked up my dress and ran to the door, numbly pulling on the handle but it wouldn't open. Caesare stopped my frantic movement with one hand, calmly turning the key.

'Back to the house and go to your room. You need to lie down and sleep. Then you'll be fine, Luci,' he told me as he ran his hands through his hair.

'You ...'

I stared at him, he looked calm, unruffled. Somehow he had fastened his breeches and there seemed to be no evidence that he had sinned with me. Nothing at all showed on his clothing or his expression. As I pulled open the door he stopped me again. Yanking me into his embrace Caesare held me to him. Afraid to refuse I stood in his arms until eventually he let go.

'You'll be fine,' he whispered, and his voice trembled.

I hurried from the library and the corridor was filled with empty, shuttered, laughing eyes instead of closed doors. And the next day, the evidence and stains of my defilement was washed away in the laundry of the *Palazzo*. That day the innocent child died and Caesare's sexual obsession with me began.

Guilt

Caesare avoided me at first. Our relationship had never been close, but I knew he must share the guilt I felt. What had happened between us was wrong and it could never occur again. A return to any form of normality seemed unlikely, although we had to exist in the same home and at least be pleasant to each other in front of everyone else.

At dinner one evening, some weeks later, I found him staring at me, a peculiar look in his eyes. I quickly averted mine. The teasing between us had stopped completely now. He no longer made remarks to get a rise out of me. I was surprised that no one else seemed to notice. Life in the Borgia world appeared to be the same to everyone but me.

'You would not believe the things I am asked for,' Father said, pointing his knife down the table at his mistress Guila Farnese, who had long since replaced my mother, Giovanna Dei Cattani, and I had lived in her household for three years now. Guila was sweet and pretty and always kind, even when Father was not present. For this I was always grateful to her.

'Do tell us, my love,' Guila smiled at Father.

'Today a peasant woman in the street during my march ...' He chewed a piece of beef fervently before continuing. '... shouts to me, "bless me with children". Guila, the woman was a hag,' he laughed. 'No miracle in the world could even bless her with a husband.'

I laughed at this, as I did all of Father's stories, as I glanced around the table to see the reaction of others. Caesare still stared at me. My smile froze. His eyes raped me. His expression burnt me. He appeared captivated by the laughter that choked in my throat.

'Did you give her a blessing, Father?' I forced my smile back in place, and turned my head back to face my Father.

'Well, I waved my hands above her, but I wouldn't insult our good Lord by asking him to allow this witch to produce hideous offspring.'

'Father, have you thought anymore about Luci's marriage?' Caesare enquired and the smile fell from my Father's face.

'You know that at some time she must be wed, Caesare. We don't want our darling girl to be left unmarried now do we?'

'She is still very young though, Father. Surely there's no need to hurry? There may yet be better matches to be made.'

I looked intently at my brother as he argued my case for me. It seemed there were advantages to the change in our relationship and I couldn't help the surge of gratitude that blossomed inside my chest like a morning daisy, full of hope that the sun will shine. I waited, hoping to grow and be free of the burden of roots.

'That may be true. However, you must trust that I have it on high authority that this is a good match. Lucrezia is a desirable prospect now. She is young, strong, healthy and beautiful.'

'Prospect? Lucrezia is a prospect? How coldly you put it, Father. But as her brother, and the second in this household, I am naturally concerned that she is to be married to a man that none of us know. What kind of man is he? Will he be kind to her? We heard he was a Spaniard.'

I was shocked by this. It had never occurred to me that the man might not be kind to me, and I had never considered his origins, because all along I had believed that Father would again change his mind.

'I know him,' Father answered, 'and I can manipulate this to my own needs.'

He turned to me then, his brown eyes serious and firm. 'Sometimes we must do what duty requires of us, Lucrezia. And that duty may not always be pleasant for a woman. But at least he is a young man and this may make you feel a little reassured.'

'But, Father,' Caesare interrupted. 'He is Spanish! How can any of us bear the thought of losing her overseas?' Caesare's eyes were raw as he met my wide-eyed stare. His voice grew soft as he spoke. 'How can you imagine never seeing Luci? Waking in the morning, knowing her smile will be given elsewhere and may never grace our table, our drawing room, our lives, again.'

I felt hypnotised by his words. I heard a passion in them that both frightened and excited me. For a moment he stared at me across the table and I felt caught in his gaze, unable to break the contact.

Father slammed his hand down on the table, violating the spell Caesare had me under. Silence deafened me. I was aware that we were all looking to the head of the table waiting for his response. Waiting as if for judgement. I wondered briefly if he had noticed the change in my brother then. Father was worldly wise, maybe he could tell that we had sinned. My cheeks reddened with guilt as my Father's eyes flicked from one to the other of us.

'It is the last I will say on the matter, Caesare. My will is law in this household and in all of Rome. I will not be questioned.' His voice was firm but barely above a whisper and we knew that when he spoke this way he was at his most furious.

Caesare knew better than to enrage Father further and he fell silent. His eyes flicked briefly in my direction and seemed both pained and angry. We continued eating as a family: solid and united under our Father's rule, even when that rule went against our own wishes and needs. Father was Pope. He was the law. He had ultimate power over us as the head of our household. And I, as a woman, had even less say. The law would uphold his right to marry me to anyone he chose. If I refused I could be cast out on the streets to an unknown fate. Until that moment refusal had never even occurred to me. After all, this was sixteenth century Rome and no woman went against her husband or father. I imagined the possible consequences; my Father's raised hand coming down across my face. I saw myself thrown out into the courtyard dressed in rags. I shuddered as any hope of freedom crumbled away and died. I envisaged myself as a daisy, failing to flourish as ice-cold rain beat it down into the mud.

'Are you cold?' Guila asked kindly.

'No.' I shook my head, my gaze flicking to my Father as he ate enthusiastically, clearly giving me no more thought. I had lost my appetite.

'You may use my shawl if you like.'

I met her eyes and for the first time I beheld sympathy. Guila had always been pleasant to me, but somewhat distant. She wasn't my mother and had never made any attempt to replace her. But she loved my Father and had at least tried to care for us. She, as a woman, also knew what the rule of a lover or husband meant. She was, although willing, as much a prisoner of her destiny as I.

'I'm fine, thank you.'

She smiled at me and I looked down at my plate feeling even more certain that the marriage would happen. Her behaviour was a further sign of my fate being sealed. I placed my fork down and took a sip of wine. I didn't want to marry. I was afraid. What if my new husband knew on our wedding night that his bride was not a virgin? How would I ever explain that to my Father? I looked again at Father as he scooped a few more pieces of meat onto his plate and consumed several glasses of wine as he ate. He seemed oblivious to my fears. Or maybe he just didn't care. A daughter could be an asset and a burden. And the right marriage was the ultimate goal. If he believed that this was the right match, then it was decided.

Dinner ended and Guila and I stood, curtseying to Father. Then I followed Guila out of the dining room.

'Thank you for trying,' I whispered, as I passed Caesare who stood respectfully as we left the room.

He looked into my eyes, his expression unfathomable. 'Let's go riding tomorrow morning, Luci.'

I left the room without further comment as the brandy decanter was opened and the men began to talk politics. I felt, as I always did in those moments, intensely curious. Their intellectual conversations interested me far more than sitting in the drawing room sewing with Guila. Being sent away always annoyed me, and I often wondered what discussions I had missed. The mystery of men was already drawing me closer, yet I recognised the imbalance of a woman's place in the world, and that I was powerless to argue or protest. Therefore if my Father wanted me to marry, then I would have to. Maybe my brother could help to persuade him. I was infinitely grateful that Caesare had at least tried to help and it never occurred to me that there might be a price to pay.

Incest

I met him in the courtyard. He stood patiently holding the reins of both of our horses. I noted the absence of the groom, couldn't fathom it. It was not how Caesare usually prepared for his morning ride. Often there were several menservants in tow.

'We aren't hunting today then, brother?' I asked.

'No.'

He held out his hand to steady me as I stepped up onto a low stool and mounted my horse. My side-saddle was made of the softest leather and had been a present from Father some months previous. Straightening my riding habit to cover my legs, I became aware that Caesare was watching me. I covered my bare ankle quickly and reached for the reins. But he held them fast for a moment forcing me to stare into his eyes.

'Luci ...'

The intensity of his expression worried me and I began to feel that riding with him was a very bad idea.

'Caesare, I do not feel inclined to go riding now after all.'

His hand on my waist stayed any attempt to dismount.

'Of course you do,' he answered simply. 'I have a beautiful picnic organised for us in a lovely spot just outside the city. You surely won't allow the provisions to go to waste, will you? With all the poverty we see in the streets, it is hardly a Christian thing to do, is it? And I need to speak with you about Father's plans.'

His eyes became veiled as he released my reins. He turned and gracefully mounted his horse. I felt I could do nothing more than follow him as he spurred his horse on out of the courtyard and into the busy street outside.

Caesare rode for the south gate, barely glancing back to see if I followed. Little did I know that this was the first of many adventures I would allow him to take me on. We galloped at break-neck speed and, as we approached the gate, the watch recognised us and waved us through without hesitation. I found myself racing over the countryside in pursuit of my wild older brother. The race sped up my heart and the recklessness of his behaviour did, as always, inspire me to urge my horse on behind him.

It was a hot day. The sun shone unrelenting. It felt good to be outside, feeling the wind whip through my hair and over my face, warm but cooling. Even the heavy clothing I wore felt light as my horse, Paradiso, galloped. I felt the tensions of the past few weeks flow away with the breeze. All would be fine. Caesare would help me convince Father not to force this marriage on me, and Father would see that it wasn't the right thing to do.

On the main stretch we passed a peasant leading an old horse pulling a cart laden with bales of hay. The man stopped when he saw us and bowed, his eyes cast down. Caesare glared at him as though contemplating punishment but then spurred his horse onwards and I followed as we seemed to gallop faster still. I glanced back briefly at the man. He had fallen to his knees and was trembling as though he had narrowly missed losing his soul to the Devil.

Caesare slowed after we had been riding hard for over half an hour. I felt fatigued but invigorated and reining in, I noticed that both our horses were foaming slightly at the mouth. They needed to drink and rest after such a hard ride.

'This way,' he said, indicating the fine forest beside us. 'I discovered a beautiful clearing here a few days ago. There's a stream running through it.'

We wove in through the trees, side by side at first, and then I dropped behind him as the woodland thickened. I felt tense, my heart and breath still quickened from the ride. I patted Paradiso's neck; she was sweating from the ride. Caesare glanced back at me, smiling and relaxed. I felt my nerves calm as I followed him deeper into the woods but inside my head was a nagging doubt that I couldn't shake.

The clearing was suddenly upon us. In the centre, just as he'd promised, lay a picnic cloth. It was spread out over the grass with huge cushions scattered on it. I felt reassured by the familiar faces of the servants from the house who stood by, ready to wait on us. The hamper was open and champagne was poured as we dismounted. The groom rushed forward to take the horses which he led to the stream and later tethered to the cart they'd used to bring the picnic. I immediately felt safe once more. I shook my head, smiling slightly at the thought of my suspecting Caesare of some evil design.

'This looks beautiful,' I said sitting down on the cloth. A servant rushed forward and held out a glass to me. I found that the wine was still chilled despite the heat of the day.

'Yes. It does,' Caesare replied taking a glass himself and sipping.

I discovered I was hungry and the spread of cold meats, fruit and cheese with fresh bread made my mouth water. It felt so civilised. All provided by the family serving staff. It felt so normal.

'So, you spoke to Father again last night?' I asked.

'Yes.'

Caesare's glass was refilled. He drank from it as the servant placed the bottle down beside him and backed away. Caesare looked around at the remaining servants. 'Leave us.'

The groom and servants dispersed, taking with them the horses and the cart that had brought the food. I began to stand, panic surging through my head and for a moment my vision blurred as fear lunged inside my heart at the thought of being alone with him. My skirt caught in the heels of my riding boots, tripping me until I tumbled back down onto the cloth beside my brother.

'What are you doing?' he asked calmly. 'I sent them away so that they cannot hear our conversation.'

I stared at Caesare. He seemed sincere but I still remembered too well our time alone in the library. Even so, I paused in my effort to rise and waited for him to explain further.

'They are devoted to Father,' he continued. 'It would appear disloyal if he were to learn we were plotting against him, wouldn't it?'

His argument seemed so plausible. I sat down again and my brother refilled my glass.

'Really Luci, you are incredibly nervous these days.'

I flushed. I was embarrassed by my lack of trust. I swigged the champagne trying to ease my nervous state. Putting down the now-empty glass I smoothed my jacket down and tried to appear composed. Did Caesare feel we could just forget our indiscretion in the library? Maybe he felt that by helping me avoid this unexpected marriage he could make amends.

'I'm sorry.'

Caesare filled my glass again. 'Don't be. I wouldn't trust me either.' He laughed then and it was infectious. I laughed also, but it was nervous energy.

As the day wore on I found myself relaxing as we talked. Leaning against the cushions I nibbled cake from the basket and watched lazily as Caesare replenished my glass once more.

'I think I can persuade him to change his plans,' he said casually.

'Really? How?' I asked, sitting up.

'It won't be easy. But I do have some pull with Father, you know. He didn't like me challenging him in front of Guila last night though, so I need to be more subtle. After all, I really would hate it if you married the Spaniard.'

'Me too. I want to marry for love.'

Caesare laughed. 'All young girls imagine that, Luci. It's very rarely a reality though. Most are married for wealth and political gain.'

'I know,' I replied. 'I'm not as stupid as you might think.'

'I know you're not stupid. In fact I think you are highly

intelligent. Maybe you could even be my intellectual equal, with guidance.'

I blushed with pleasure. Caesare had never spoken to me like this before. I had always been his silly younger sister. Yet now he was treating me like an adult and speaking to me on a different level. Another bottle appeared from the basket and he popped the cork, topping up both of our glasses. I felt relaxed, the sun was soothing and I lay down. Caesare reclined too, his head rested on his hand as he lay on his side watching me calmly as we talked.

'It's about time you admitted it,' I giggled. 'Tell me, I've always wanted to know ...'

'What?' he asked.

'What do you and Father talk about when we leave?'

'Politics.'

'Guila says that.'

'Women.'

I looked at him, surprised, and he smiled slowly, playfully. 'You're teasing me.'

'No, not at all.'

'What else?'

'Religion. But he always talks about that at some point,' Caesare laughed. 'And of course, we talk about family matters.'

'So, you talked to Father about me last night?'

Caesare stretched out flat on his back, his arms folded under his head, and gazed up into the blue sky. I tried to wait but his silence irritated me.

'Well?'

I sat up. Caesare's eyes were closed, his mouth and face relaxed. He had fallen asleep. I lay back against a cushion, my head was spinning from the champagne and I closed my eyes, dozing a little to pass the time while I waited for him to wake and talk to me some more.

The warm sun filtered through the trees as I drifted into a relaxed floating vision. My heart rate slowed and I slept.

I dreamed of a lover, kissing me, stroking me as I lay stretched in his embrace. The memory of the excitement I'd felt in the library remained with me and I craved the feeling again as I opened to this mystery lover's mouth and tongue that licked, kissed and sucked me tenderly in that sensitive spot.

I felt a cool breeze on my bare legs. The illusion was so vivid, I imagined him opening my bodice, laying bare my breasts as his mouth found my nipple until I groaned louder. And then the pressure was gone, the touch had left me.

I woke and found Caesare stripping away his clothing as he stood over me. I was naked; my clothing lay in a neat pile beside me. I felt stunned as the remains of his clothes fell next to mine and he lay beside me. His lips and tongue trailed across my breasts and I floated back into the dream state, captivated by the pleasure of it.

He gasped against my bare nipple. 'So beautiful.'

I was awake this time and aware of what was happening, but desire drove me. I wanted that feeling again, wanted my orgasm to gush against his mouth.

'Oh my God,' I groaned.

I couldn't stop him now, even if I had wanted, and I didn't want. I needed him. Blood rushed to my face, my nails dug into his buttocks. I whimpered softly at first, but my cries grew louder as we approached the moment of fulfilment. As I came with him I knew we should never do this again, but wondered how I could ever resist him.

'I love you Luci,' he gasped, his head against my breast as he poured inside me.

His words terrified me, but not as much as the pained obsessive expression that filled his eyes as he gazed down into my face.

I turned my head away and glanced at the empty bottles of champagne. What had I done? What was going to become of us? I stroked his hair as he wrapped his arms around me and cried. I knew then, he was more afraid than I was. The act had excited me in a different way; it made me feel strong. It was as though his desire for me gave me a power over my brother. I think this is why I allowed our relationship to continue.

Lover Revealed

I remain silent as Lucrezia stops speaking. She stands and stretches like a cat. She looks out of the window onto the street as a passing Mercedes slows and turns into the drive next door. I realise how difficult this story is for her to tell, but I find even harder the revelation that she encouraged her brother; that she wanted him to make love to her; that she willingly entered into an incestuous relationship with him.

'Are you okay?' I ask.

She sighs deeply, running her hand across her forehead. 'I need to stop for a while.'

'Of course. Can I get you anything?' It is ironic how our roles are reversed. I see that this is not lost on her as she gives me an amused smile.

'I've never voiced this,' she says, wrapping her arms around her body.

'Yes,' I agree. 'But maybe you needed to?'

She nods.

'My life was very different then, as you can see. But I shan't attempt to justify my actions, merely express the facts.'

'We have both lived many lives; I'm not here to make any judgement.'

My mobile phone rings suddenly in my pocket. It is a quirky tune, *Black And Gold* by a singer called Sam Sparro. Lilly put it on my phone because she loved the song. We'd danced to it one night in a hotel room in Rome, as the video played on MTV.

'And now we are back in the present.' Lucrezia laughs, breaking my momentary reverie.

I smile at her while retrieving my phone from my pocket. It's Lilly. She'll be wondering where I am. We have barely been apart in over a year. And I lied to her about where I was going. I stare at the screen as it rings.

'Aren't you going to answer?'

I shake my head, unsure what to do. It stops ringing as I am about to press receive. I stare blankly at the missed call message.

'Mmmm,' Lucrezia smiles. 'She'll be wondering what you're doing.'

I stand and walk to the door. 'Maybe I should come back later?'

'Why not bring her?' Lucrezia looks at me sincerely. 'I've known about her all along, since her re-birth. I felt it.'

I open my mouth to speak but cannot find words. Lilly is my secret, my lover, my companion. How do I discuss that with someone who amounts to my ex-lover, however briefly?

'She doesn't know about you,' I say finally.

'Ah.'

I flounder, wondering what to do and my phone rings again, shaking me from my confusion. I answer quickly this time.

'Hi.'

'Hi,' she answers uncertainly. 'Is something wrong?'

'No, my darling. I just missed your call, that's all.'

She doesn't believe me. 'Oh?'

'Have you checked in for us yet?' I ask, wondering if I sound too perky.

'Yes. There now. Waiting for you.' Her tone drops, and I respond immediately to the sexual urgency in her voice. 'Have you dealt with the "business" you had to attend to yet? Only, like I said, I'm waiting.' She hangs up, leaving me dangling, and I ache for her as always.

I close my phone and turn to Lucrezia.

'You have to go,' she says.

'Yes. But I need to know more. We have barely touched the surface of your story.'

'True.' She shivers. 'But, it will be long in the telling, I feel.'

I glance at my phone again, feeling the urge to turn it off, and sit again waiting patiently for her story to unfold.

'But it can wait,' Lucrezia continues. 'Lovers often don't like to.'

I sit, making the decision. 'I'm not ready to go yet. It will all be fine if I take my time. I'm not so insecure to think that she will leave me if I'm a few hours late.'

Lucrezia laughs, then sits opposite me. 'Send her a text to say you'll be delayed then. That's what they do in this century and it seems so acceptable, doesn't it?'

I smile. We understand each other so well and our mutual contempt for the manners of the modern world is just one small thing we share. We have a history together, after all. I suppose more than that, we *are* history. I switch off my phone.

'I will stay a little longer if you feel you can continue.'

'Good. But now it's your turn. I would like to know about your life. I want to know about her.'

'Lilly,' I state.

'A beautiful name,' Lucrezia says and I meet her eyes. Eyes that are so like my lover's that it makes my heart ache.

'She is a lot like you.'

'Will I meet her?' Lucrezia asks.

'Soon.'

Loving Lilly

'Luxury is just too easy to get used to.'

I lean back into the comfortable leather passenger seat of Lilly's shiny black Aston Martin convertible. The hardtop roof is slicked back into the boot. Lilly's hair writhes around the headrest of the driver's seat in the wind. She likes the car despite her aversion to ostentation. I smile briefly at the irony and at the change in her.

'Yes. It is.' I reach a hand over to her lovely slender leg, stroke down the cream coloured skirt until I find the bare flesh I'm seeking.

'Behave. Unless you want me to crash?' Lilly laughs, throwing back her honey hair.

She's had it straightened, cut shorter, part of the change of image for our new existence. We are Mr and Mrs Gabriele Caccini. After years of hiding it, I felt it might be interesting to use my original name. My sources at the passport offices, the birth and marriage registrars, various bank clerks who are well paid to move money electronically for me, don't care. They would never even assume that this was my real identity. My money buys real documents, real identities and real loyalty.

Technology is an amazing thing. It has become easier, not harder, to be who I wish. All I need to do is to create records of movements, credit history, bogus trips through customs. So straightforward. So easy when you have the money, because in any century that is all that most people care about.

My hand slips further up her thigh, finds the soft folds beneath. She rarely wears underwear, but something silky greets my fingertips. She squirms, a smile playing across her face.

'Please...'

I pull my hand away, taking pity on the other road users. A crash will not kill us, but it may harm others and draw unnecessary attention to us. My fingers tingle from touching her skin and I raise them slowly to my lips, licking her essence from the tips.

'You're outrageous,' she says, but her eyes are on fire with mutual lust for me.

'I know.'

She brushes her skirt back in place taking a deep gulping breath. 'I'm still not used to it.'

'I don't know, you seem to have a lot of skill.' I smile.

Her look quells me. 'You know what I mean. Your touch is electric.'

'Yours is to me.'

'It feels different then? To when you have been with others?'

I raise an eyebrow, surprised. Is my darling jealous? I like the thought.

'There are no other women that could compare to you, Lilly.'

A slight smile fights to spread from the corners of her mouth. It's the expression she has when she doesn't want me to know she's pleased with me. We've been together for a year now, and I've never been happier. I've lived a hundred lives; changed my name, my hair, my age, my religion, all to suit the style and conventions of the time. But now I find I have a future with a beautiful woman who loves me. This is a new experience. This is all I have ever wanted.

Lilly steers the car around a sharp bend. I watch her face as she concentrates. Even her serious expressions are compellingly addictive. She is the biggest rush I have ever had.

'Are you going to explain?' she asks.

I don't reply.

'You've been dragging me all over Europe for the last few months. It's clear that we are supposed to be looking for something ... or someone. And then you disappear for hours and don't tell me where you are. I could be very suspicious and suspect there is another woman.'

I keep my eyes on the road ahead, but feel her looking at me. I don't flush with guilt. A lifetime of experience hiding my emotions pays its dividends at that moment. We join the long line of traffic that takes us around Piccadilly towards our hotel. Lilly navigates the road perfectly and I relax again in my seat, hoping she won't pursue her earlier questions. I'm too uncertain of everything.

Lilly sighs. Her irritation permeates the air like a gust of invisible dust.

'Okay. Don't tell me then.'

A black limousine swerves in front of us, almost taking off the front bumper, but Lilly negotiates the road like an experienced racing driver. Like her other instincts, her reflexes are faultless. She knows I am holding back from her. But what can I tell her when I am uncertain of the facts myself? Lucrezia has yet to finish her story and I have not yet understood why our origins are so important to the success of reproduction. Or, what diabolical creature we encountered that sucked the very energy from our bodies by its mere proximity.

Lilly pulls up outside the hotel, jumping from her seat as she snatches the keys from the ignition and throws them to the concierge in one fluid movement.

I place a fifty pound note in his hand on top of the keys.

'Why is it we're back in Manchester?' Lilly asks again, her smile cynical. 'You did say you wouldn't set foot in this town after last time.'

'Yes. I also recall that I added "unless I was going to finish off the flea-bitten Nate and break more than his grubby finger bones".'

I feel myself scowling at the thought of Nate and Steve and their meddling. On my first visit here I posed as a student at Manchester University. I had been stalking my latest fascination, Carolyn. Who was, unfortunately, dating a lout called Steve.

Steve and his pierced and tattooed friend, Nate (of the unwashed variety) meddled a little too closely in my affairs. In a moment of anger I revealed my vampiric nature. This, of course, meant that Lilly and I had to leave immediately. I swore I'd return and finish the job one day.

Lilly laughs, linking her arm in mine as the lift doors close and we begin our ascent to the top floor. I find myself grinning back at her flowing smile, before I lean in to kiss her blood-filled lips. She giggles under my mouth. She always has a way of manipulating me from my moods and her über feminine giggle makes my pulse race in a far more satisfying way than it ever has. This time, however, I sense something else in her laughter; an undercurrent. My old paranoia, my fear of losing her, kicks in once more and I scan her beautiful face looking for any sign that she doesn't love me.

'What's so funny?'

'You. Your elephant memory and lust for vendetta. But I am curious a little if Carolyn and Steve got jiggy, eventually.' She laughs. 'She was so annoyingly virginal.'

'I remember.' I leer and Lilly punches my arm.

The lift jolts as it stops. We walk a short way down the dimly lit corridor until I see the room number that corresponds with the swipe key in my hand. I take Lilly's hand in mine and smile at her.

'Seriously though. Why here? Why now?'

'I'll explain everything soon, darling.' As soon as it becomes clear in my own head.

'Thought we weren't doing secrets anymore.'

Secrets. Now, there's a word. For the past year we've travelled. A trip back to Italy taking in Venice, Rome, Florence, Turin. All cities where I could search for Lucrezia or my family line, although of course Lilly thought it was merely a tour to bring her up to speed with my past. Now she knows everything. How my uncle was Giulio Caccini, the composer and musician who invented Opera. She learned of my passionate obsession with my cousin Francesca, Giulio's daughter. Then, as I broke down in a hotel in Verona, I revealed how I loved my children so much I gave them up for their own safety. Lilly knows my secrets – mostly. She doesn't know that the travel was an excuse to search; search for the woman who made me into a vampire over four hundred years ago.

'It's complicated.'

Lilly frowns as I swipe the card down the door scanner and the green light flicks on to allow us access to the room. I reach inside and flip the light switch out of habit, even though neither of us needs the light. We can see perfectly well in the dark.

The room lights up. It's a suite. We always do everything in style and despite Lilly's aversion to luxury she has begun to come around to my way of thinking. This part of the room is a sitting area. There is a huge flat screen television facing a beige *chaise longue*, which is both alike and unlike the black and red ones we saw in the reception as we arrived. The hotel is a gothic dream for those of us who like it ... and I do, I must admit.

Lilly throws her handbag down on the *chaise longue* as I go to investigate the rest of the suite. To the right is a door that leads into a toilet, black and white, beautifully designed; I smile in approval as I look through the door. Lilly kicks off her shoes and puts her feet up on the coffee table, but I refuse to let her unladylike behaviour bait me as I head through the archway that leads to the bedroom. Here there is another television at the bottom of the bed on a rich mahogany unit with a DVD player and stereo: all the media conveniences any visitor could want. The bed is plush, covered in rich brown and cream cloth, with cushions resting on the brown velvet-covered headboard. Either side of the bed are two mahogany side tables. To my left is another mahogany unit, bigger than the one holding the television. I open it to find a fridge and safe. As I close it I spot two more doors, one leading to a full sized bathroom, again in black and white, which contains a bath as well as separate double shower cubicle. Good. We'll make use of both ...

I see my hand luggage in the corner and lift it onto the bed. I withdraw my favoured candles to place them around the room. In the reception room, I hear Lilly turn on the television. The blare of different pieces of music and snatches of speech echoes through the wall as she flicks through the channels. I reach inside my pocket to pull out a lighter. Flicking it alight I go from one candle to the other until they are all lit. Twelve of them, all scented with vanilla.

Lilly peeps in through the alcove as I open the mini-bar and remove a bottle of chilled champagne. Her eyes grow round as she looks at the candlelit room.

'What's all this?'

The champagne cork pops free with a shrug of my thumb and forefinger and the foam bursts forth faster than the tiny glass can cope with it.

'A celebration. We've been together a year.'

It seems obsurd that we can gain so much pleasure out of the thought of drinking Champagne. It is a luxury after all. We can't get drunk, a momentary tingle is all we will experience from the wine, but still a tiny flush appears in Lilly's pale cheeks. It is both pleasure and vague embarrassment.

'Of course I know that,' she whispers. 'Shocked that you do.'

'Why?' Her blush calls to me; my cock feels like it is drawn in her direction by some will of its own.

'Because, I guess it just surprises me that you have such awareness of time, when you have an abundance of it.'

She moves into the room as I had hoped she would and glides to the bed, sitting down on the edge; her cream wrap-over skirt parts and I glimpse the flesh coloured hold-up stocking top that I adore so much. She makes no move to cover her bare thigh and I fall forward, hurriedly placing the champagne bottle and glass on the bedside table. My hand is on her leg and she runs her fingers swiftly up my arm, squeezing, feeling the muscles that ripple beneath the fabric of my shirt.

'Mmmm. I never tire of feeling your strength, Gabriele.'

'Now can I make love to you?' I laugh.

As Lilly falls into a deep sleep, I slip quietly out of the room.

'Doors,' she murmurs as I leave, and I love that sometimes she talks in her sleep.

Closing the suite door quietly behind me, I move into the night, heading once more for Lucrezia and her tales of the past.

Affair

Caesare took me riding often and our affair continued unchecked, unnoticed by anyone. Sometimes, he would sneak into my room at night and make love to me while everyone slept. At first, not even our father suspected that our new friendship was unseemly, was anything more than a normal brother-sister relationship..

During the day we played games like children, and I suppose we were. I was only fifteen and Caesare just a few years older. I took to dressing as a boy. We'd ride out of the gates, while I was disguised as a squire, riding astride a horse. Rumours of our exploits began to be whispered in scandalised voices in the halls of the Vatican. My nosy servant girl giggled when she caught me changing from my boy's clothing into a more appropriate evening dress of silk and lace. But it didn't stop. I think, in some way, I was in love with Caesare, certainly infatuated. More than anything, I was enjoying the freedom that our relationship gave me.

We rode together every day and then we would return to the grove. Caesare would bring ecstatic cries from me, as he loved me over and over until we were both exhausted. The afternoon would blend into evening as we lay together under the sun, our skin softly browning. My natural olive hue deepened.

'It's most unladylike,' Guila pointed out. She sent me creams and powders one evening. 'Perhaps you should consider wearing a veil when you are outside?'

I looked at Guila closely, wondering if this observation meant she knew what was happening between Caesare and I. As she bowed her head back to her embroidery, I had no sense that she thought anything was amiss. I took to powdering my face, and as we made love in the grove, I encouraged Caesare to lie with me in the shade instead of the sun.

I was a willing participant, although I was not naive enough to believe it could go on forever. Some days I thought that one day we would both tire of it. We would return to our former lives as brother and sister, as if nothing had ever happened. At other times I prayed it wouldn't end for the love and lust were so intense I could not imagine my life without it.

'We must be careful,' he warned.

Caesare often did not take his own advice and sometimes at dinner he gazed longingly at me. If we were in a social gathering, his eyes would follow me as I circled the room. Once or twice I thought I observed Guila looking from one to the other of us and I was afraid. I would cool my expression and still my body language, concentrating on my needlepoint, while trying to disregard Caesare's hurt expression.

'Please, Caesare, you must understand that we are at times too obvious with each other. What if we are discovered?' I told him more than once. 'Father would ...'

'It won't happen. Why should it? We have been careful.'

'Not careful enough sometimes,' I pointed out.

My brother chose to ignore my warnings.

'Father is not suspicious. He knows you dress as a boy. He laughed about it with me last night after dinner. He likes that you are enjoying a certain freedom.'

'Yes. Because he still intends to marry me to the Spaniard. Then I will have no freedom, no life of my own. I will have to appear a devoted wife.'

'It will never happen. Besides, I can't help how I look at you sometimes. I want you night and day, don't you know that?'

Caesare kissed my hand. He was so loving and I adored him despite the fact that I knew it was wrong. I couldn't help myself. We were caught up in some misguided fascination, which I knew one day would come to an end. Our world would change with the forthcoming marriage and so far our father had been adamant that it would go ahead.

'But, if he does marry me to this Spaniard … on the wedding night I must play the virgin in the way that you taught me.' I giggled stroking my nail down his bare chest. 'I'll be all coy and scared and tremble.'

'No. I couldn't bear it,' Caesare gasped, sitting beside me on my bed. 'I could never allow another man to touch you, to have you. You're mine, Luci. You belong to me and no other can have you.'

He kissed me and a shiver ran down my spine as though some evil omen or curse had been spoken. He held me to him, as though he could mould me to him forever. I pushed him away.

'Ouch. Please Caesare, not so rough! We must be realistic. You're my brother and the scandal would kill Father. He's determined. The wedding will happen next month.'

'Then let's leave.'

I stared at him, uncertain as to his meaning and proclamation. 'Leave? And go where?'

'I have been saving money, we could go anywhere, Luci. We could live as man and wife, change our names. Who would know?'

I sat up, swinging my bare legs over the edge of the bed. Caesare could be so naive and childlike sometimes. It was hard to believe he was the elder of us. I knew Father could and would find us anywhere in Rome, anywhere in Italy. He was the Pope. His power stretched over most of the world. I stepped naked from our bed and reached for a robe.

'Oh no!' Caesare gasped suddenly and I spun to look at him.
'What?'

'Your belly. Oh my God. I've been so foolish.'

I glanced down at my slightly swollen stomach, uncomprehending. I had thought little of the minor weight gain and the discomfort of sickness in the morning. I had put it down to nerves.

'I think you're with child.'

Scandal

At first I was afraid and hurt that he might use my possible pregnancy as a reason for abandoning me. After all he said he loved me, and that we should run away together. But he'd lied. Following that night, Caesare's fear kept him from my bed and my company for more than a week. He became listless, locking himself away in his quarters. I was told that he also sent the servants away when they offered him food. It had never occurred to me that my brother was weak in any sense. His behaviour was a huge disappointment. I waited anxiously for news every day, even put a letter under his door in an attempt to encourage him to talk to me.

The household buzzed with fears that my brother was ill, and my worried pallor became noticeable. Rumours of fever and plague spread amongst the servants; rumours that Father could not allow to continue. So, one morning, he sent for a physician to examine Caesare.

'He has a fever,' the doctor told Father, 'and he seems to be in a severe state of agitation. The fever itself seems minor. He must be encouraged to eat and drink again if he is to recover quickly.'

'Did he express why he was distressed?' Father asked.

'No.'

'I will have to go and speak with him myself then. Look in on my daughter,' Father requested. 'She's not herself either; her pallor is a great cause for concern to us all.'

I refused to let him examine me. 'My brother is sick. Father has plans for my wedding shortly. Of course I feel worried!' I snapped.

The doctor put my nerves down to 'virginal anxiety' and suggested that the wedding be postponed, at least until Caesare recovered from his illness. So Caesare had gained some respite for us. His fever was genuine and I began to grow more and more concerned about his health and his state of mind. His avoidance of me continued and, much to my horror, I realised one morning that his suspicions were true. I really was pregnant and I would have to face this alone.

I spent sleepless nights tossing and turning and worrying what could happen. I was certain that my father would send me away. Maybe I would be publicly shamed. Caesare would no longer protect me from my father, how could he? He would probably deny any involvement. If I were to accuse my own brother it would only be worse for me. For what kind of sick mind would devise a lie of incest?

Tortured, I stopped eating. Maybe if I died it would be the best thing for everyone. No matter how hard my handmaid tried, she could not get me to eat or drink.

A few days into my enforced starvation, Caesare came to me. It was in the middle of the night. I was feverish, dehydrated, and I thought I was hallucinating.

I dreamt of a corridor of many doors, all made of different materials. And every one I tried was locked. Before me shone a bright entrance that bulged and bowed as if an immense weight were pushing against it from inside.

'I thought I could stay away, deny everything,' he said. 'But I can't be without you, Luci.'

He climbed into my bed and began to stroke my weak body, while I lay under him, unresponsive. I felt him harden, his touch became more insistent, but I turned away from him.

'What is it? What's wrong with you?'

I didn't answer and he sat up, reaching for a pitcher of water, he poured a glass and forced it to my lips.

'Stupid girl. What have you done to yourself?'

I croaked, spitting the water back out. 'It's better for everyone this way.'

'Not better for me.'

'You went away, you let me down.'

Caesare pushed the glass to my lips once more and I swallowed, choking on the liquid. My body was so parched, it responded involuntarily and I gulped down large amounts before he stopped me. 'Slowly.'

He lay beside me, holding me. Occasionally sitting up to bring me more water.

'I did have a minor ailment. But I wanted to think about things. Make plans,' he told me.

'Plans?' I turned to face him again. Hope blossomed in my chest, pushing away the fear and loneliness of the previous weeks. Caesare would run away with me, as he had promised. That had to be the only solution open to us now.

'Yes. I have been to see an apothecary. He's making a potion that will help you abort. Our problem is solved, Luci.'

My limbs became paralysed. I lay stiff and afraid as Caesare explained the effects of the potion. I felt sick.

'And then we can carry on as before. Of course you may be sick for a while. But that will only help our plans with postponing the wedding ...'

'Get out,' I said pushing him away. 'Get out and never come near me again.'

'Luci. Be sensible. You know this can be the only resolution.'

'You said you loved me. You said you wanted to run away with me, how can this have changed things?'

'Luci, we don't want a baby right now. How can we possibly? But later, when we can leave, when we can pretend to be man and wife, then it may be possible. Don't you see your confinement will be a hindrance to our plans?'

I closed my eyes. I wanted to sleep and never wake.

'I hate you. Go away.'

He wouldn't leave.

Not until his lust was satisfied.

He forced himself on me, rutting like an animal, knowing he could pour his seed inside me now without further consequence. He stayed there for most of the night, taking me over and over as I remained limp and unresponsive beneath him.

In the morning I lay listless but could no longer resist the food or water offered. With the realisation that I wanted to spare the child inside me, my sense of survival prevailed. Caesare's suggestion that we murder the baby had the opposite affect. I wanted my sin to be born into the world for all to see. I wanted the world to recognise that I was a whore. Only a whore would lay with her own brother.

I quickly recovered. Father and the servants soon forgot that Caesare and I had been sick. Life seemed to return to normal. Except, I now locked my door at night. Every morning a new letter would be pushed under my door.

Luci, please. I do love you. I can't live without you.

Caesare of course was mortified by my rejection, but the more I ignored his notes, the more threatening they became.

You're a fool. Soon the world will recognise you for a whore. How stupid, when I could have helped you. Let me back in tonight and we will say no more about it. Otherwise, I will renounce you!

I avoided being alone with him at every opportunity, but sometimes he contrived to catch me unawares and it was during these moments that his anger flared the most. Even then I didn't know how terrible his rage could be.

'What do you think you're doing? The longer we leave this the harder on you it will be. Take the potion, Luci. Don't you realise how dangerous this could be if the pregnancy continues? Someone will surely notice.'

We were at a small gathering and I had gone outside to get some fresh air. It was mid-afternoon in May; the day was warm but not too hot. The garden of our host was beautifully maintained. I wandered among the flower-lined paths, looking only for some peace. It was easy to deny my circumstances in the light of day with natural beauty to distract me.

'Go to hell, brother dear,' I replied. 'I will not take the life of my child, no matter what it costs me.'

'Bitch. You endanger us both,' he cried grabbing my arm and spinning me around to look at him.

'Why are you so afraid? It is me that will bring shame on the family, not you. And Father will just send me away when he realises. At least then I will not have to wed the Spaniard. More importantly I will not have to see you again.'

I pulled my arm free, and rubbed the skin, feeling the start of bruising.

'You're naive to believe that all Father will do is send you away. He's the Pope, and you, his daughter, will be named as a whore. I'll tell him.'

'You'll tell him what? That you raped me in his library?'

'You wanted it.'

My stomach churned as I looked into his bloodshot eyes. He'd been drinking since I had rejected him. There was a darkness surrounding him. A cold, selfish glow that made me feel afraid and again that shiver ran up my spine. He looked feverish, obsessed and furious.

At that moment a group of girls my age left the house. Their excited chatter reached us. Caesare's eyes released me from their hypnotic hold to glance quickly in their direction. It gave me the opportunity to turn and walked away from him towards the small group.

'Lucrezia, join us,' shouted my friend, Alcia. 'Oh, and why don't you bring your most handsome and charming brother with you?'

I felt Caesare turn to follow, my shoulders stiffened. Alcia was always flirtatious with Caesare. He had often laughed at her interest and I wondered now what he would do. I could still feel his anger as he caught up with my fast steps across the lawn, grabbing my elbow, swinging me around once more.

'Unlock your door to me again,' he said. 'I can't bear it. I want you.'

I stared at him. 'Leave me alone, Caesare. We both knew it was a sin and now we are being punished. I am no longer your whore.'

I pulled free of him and left, hurrying towards the girls confidently. Although I didn't look back, I knew that Caesare turned on his heel and strode away in the opposite direction.

'Whatever is the matter with Caesare?' asked Alcia.

'Oh, we had a fight. He annoys me, he's so bossy.'

'I have the same problem with my brother,' Alcia replied.

Confinement

It wasn't long before Father discovered my secret.

Guila knew of course. She had suspected all along that Caesare and I were experimenting with each other. Our sudden rift was a sure sign to her that things had progressed further than they should. It was Guila who came for me, her eyes grave as she led me from my room that morning to my father's study.

'It seems I have been too lapse in my duties as a father,' he said.

I found it impossible to look at him. Father was still in his papal robes. He had just delivered a special mass.

My cheeks flushed with guilt. Caesare stood beside me, head downcast, but I didn't look at him. I felt him swaying slightly beside me as I trembled and shied away from the accusing gaze of our father.

'You were seen together,' Father continued. 'Fortunately by a loyal servant. Hence I have been able to avoid scandal.'

'Seen?' I asked my voice quivering.

Father glared at me. 'I should have named you Eve.'

So I was to be blamed. I was the temptress who led Caesare astray. I was the whore. I waited for his condemnation. Maybe we would be publicly renounced, flogged or, if Father felt strongly enough, even executed. Caesare remained as silent as I. How can we deny the truth? I felt such rage that he would stand there and let me take all of the blame. But then, how could I possibly expect anything more from him?

'I thought at first it was nothing, that Caesare would tire of his little game with you and you would have gained some experience to take into your marriage, Luci. But it seems things have gone too far.'

I felt his eyes bore into my belly. It was clear to me that Caesare had confessed to Father, had told him everything, throwing himself at his mercy in a bid to receive lesser punishment. I could not decide whether this final betrayal was vindictive because I had refused to let him return to my bed. His anger had been so intense the last time we met. He had threatened to tell Father I was pregnant, had threatened to tell him I was a whore, unless I let him in. I opened my mouth to speak, to tell Father that Caesare had raped me. He would not make me take all the blame.

I glanced at my brother and saw the bruises. Blood seeping from his lips and around his mouth, spilled over his once crisp white shirt. He swayed on his feet. He looked hurt, frail and weak. I realised then that he hadn't told on me; the truth had been *beaten* from him.

My emotions were in turmoil. I felt pain for him, fear for myself. I was unable to speak, for what defence could I offer? I was a whore; I had committed incest with my brother. The church would condemn us. The very least we could expect was exile and it was unlikely that that would be our only lot.

Father turned to me, his eyes furious. As he stepped forward, his arm raised to strike me, both Guila and Caesare moved in front of me.

'Don't hurt her. It was me! All of it my fault, Father. I told you! She was too innocent to understand what was happening,' Caesare begged. 'Please, she's with child. Don't hurt her. Punish me.'

Caesare threw himself down before our father, who stopped, shocked by the ferocity of his defence of me. His eyes skipped from Caesare to me. Guila held my shaking body against her, her eyes pleading with Father. At that moment she was more a mother to me than she had ever been.

'Please,' she begged. 'She's merely a child!'

'Take her out of my sight,' Father ordered. 'Caesare, you shall be punished.'

Guila led me away. I looked back once more at Caesare still lying at the feet of our father. Father wore a glazed, somewhat insane expression, as he turned his eyes from me to his kneeling son, who quivered as he waited for the blows to fall.

Guila took me back to my room, where I found two young servant girls packing my clothing and personal possessions into trunks. I burst into tears and Guila took my hand, sending the servants away as she laid me on my bed.

'Some brothers and sisters do learn about love together,' Guila told me. 'But never take things beyond propriety.'

'Father. . ?'

'He knows this. And all will be taken care of. He's brought your wedding date forward again.' Guila stroked my head.

'What!' I tried to sit but she forced me back down.

'Please don't be afraid. Your new husband will not be permitted to have you. The marriage will be in name only, Lucrezia, and your father will pay him well for his troubles.'

'Everyone will know,' I answered. 'My condition will become obvious soon.'

'That is why you and I are going on a trip. We'll be away for several months. It will coincide with your father's Papal duties. He needs to do a tour of Italy. All of Rome will think you are with him, but instead you will be doing your confinement in a mountain retreat.'

I fell silent. My shame would be hidden. But what of my child?

'All will be taken care of,' Guila said again.

I should have felt reassured. The sinister realisation that I needed to be hidden and 'taken care of' terrified me. I knew my father had ordered deaths for less than my shame would cause him. So what might become of me in my confinement? More importantly, what might become of my baby?

A proxy wedding ensued. This was a common occurrence and the contract stated that the marriage was not to be consummated for a year. I would remain with my family in Rome during that time. For his trouble, my new husband, Giovanni Sforza d'Aragona (a mercenary captain), would receive 31,000 ducats as a dowry; a huge sum. His own illegitimacy ensured his compliance. Making a match with the daughter of the Pope was a very good political move. He did not know that his new wife was already with child. Any future meeting with me would take place long after the birth. He was paid well for all his patience.

'What was he told?' I asked Guila.

'That your father considers you too young for consummation, but in a year it will be possible.'

'So, I'm to be given to him anyway,' I protested quietly.

'We shall see,' Guila smiled. 'Your father has the whole thing worked out.'

So on the twelfth of June I was taken from Rome, immediately after the wedding, up into the mountains and to a house in San Marino, out of the jurisdiction of Rome. And there, six months later, I gave birth to my first son.

Chapter 11 - Present

A Thief In The Night

I stare at the tears in her eyes. Why am I so surprised that Lucrezia once had humanity? Why am I so amazed that she loved her child? My arrogance has led me to believe that I was the only one who had emotions, who cared about the past. Now I am more intrigued than ever to know what happened to her to make her so bitter and cold when we first met, when she changed my life forever.

'You loved your son.'

'Yes, and like a thief in the night they took him from me. I gave him a name though, I called him Antonio; I don't know if he was called that later.'

I blink, confused. 'What happened to him?'

She shakes her head, unable to speak.

We are in a bar now, no longer at her house. Lucrezia had said she wanted a more neutral territory to tell me more. The music from the speakers is too loud and the Karaoke will start soon. It is hardly the right place to discuss the old world. It is most certainly inappropriate to reveal such raw emotion. Yet this is her chosen place. This is her appointed 'neutral'.

'Would you like to leave, go somewhere quieter?' I ask.

She blinks, looking around as though she has only just noticed the noise and the bustle. I narrow my eyes at the waiter who placed us here. Another time I would have killed him just for looking at me in the wrong way. He's arrogant and shifty and of mixed race, though I can't tell what mix. He finally brings the drinks we ordered, slamming them down on the table before us.

'Eleven pounds fifty,' he demands. I hand him the exact money. I feel no urge to reward his attitude.

As he snatches the money from my hand, clearly annoyed that I haven't tipped him, I notice he has a small tattoo on his knuckle. It is some form of Celtic symbol. It looks like a fish on a hook. Strange.

We are in a corner, not quite a booth, but out of the way and it does afford us some privacy. Lucrezia glances down at her shaking hands. She clasps the large glass of red wine she ordered. She is silent.

On the stage a Christina Aguilera wannabe takes up the mike before the intro for *Beautiful* pours from the speakers around the room. The girl sings; she's good. I feel Lucrezia move beside me and I look to her again. She sips her wine; her fingers aren't trembling anymore. Her composure seems to have returned.

'I never saw my son again,' she continues. 'One glimpse they allowed me, and then they took him. I have no idea what happened to him after that. Guila assured me he would be raised by a loving family. At first I didn't believe her, but then she pointed out that Father's religion would never allow him to murder a child.'

'Yes. Not surprising really. You couldn't keep him because your father could hardly have you acknowledge the child's existence. I suspect you would have, wouldn't you?'

She nods. 'Of course, Guila tried to reassure me that it was the best thing. She said that there would be something wrong with the baby. Modern science would probably hold to that anyway, that my relationship was too close to Caesare. Our child would likely be retarded or deformed. But he looked perfect, Gabi. He was beautiful. If I close my eyes I can still see him, wrapped in a white sheet. He had green eyes. Just like mine.'

I take her hand, stroke my thumb over her cold fingers and note with interest that her aura does not provoke the reaction in me that Lilly's does. She feels like my sister, not a lover. I ache for her loss because it is so relative to my own. Yet Lilly's love has helped me so much to come to terms with the past. Maybe I can help Lucrezia now.

'Life returned to normal for a while,' she begins again. 'Of course, when my family refused to give me over to Giovanni a year later, he grew angry. His accusations of incest were so accurate. Even though he didn't know for certain. He suspected Father, and then later, when he'd barged into St Peter's and found me in the Library with both my brother and Father, he assumed we were a den of iniquity.'

I ask her to explain 'found with' and she laughs. They had merely been talking and planning to extricate her from the marriage. Constant refusal to bed Giovanni gave him just cause to insist on an annulment. This meant of course that he could also keep the ducats he received as dowry. The Pope and his family had failed to keep their part of the agreement. Therefore Giovanni Sforza's grievance was justified. Naturally that was all part of Pope Alexander's plan.

'And Caesare?'

Lucrezia's eyes are raw as she meets my gaze. Her hand reaches up, pushing back an invisible strand of hair from her face.

'Caesare had changed beyond recognition. I had felt some loyalty to him after he defended me. I don't know what punishment befell him in my absence. But he was crueller; darker and more brooding. His expression was a continual sneer, especially when I was in the room. He came to my room the first night of my return to Rome to find himself locked out. He just couldn't accept my refusal. Of course, Giovanni was right; he could see it in my brother's eyes that day. Caesare was obsessed with me; it wasn't love anymore. He believed I belonged to him, and he wouldn't leave me alone.'

'He stalked you?'

Lucrezia nods. 'In a way. But my Father's influence protected me from him and any further contact for several years. He married me off again as soon as possible. Of course that didn't help, because Caesare's fury grew and the love he had once borne for me became twisted and warped beyond all recognition.'

'A futile flame,' I say.

'Yes. And it never burnt out.'

The Fall Of The Borgias

There were further marriages of course. Further lives that I lived in my attempts to avoid Caesare. My brother became influential and feared. No one ever went against him. Those that did, disappeared under mysterious circumstances. Father used his madness to control him.

Soon after the death of my second husband, Father quickly arranged my re-marriage. I believe he feared for me alone, with Caesare constantly in the background, trying to gain access to me at every opportunity. Maybe he knew his own life was coming to an end and he wished for me to be safe. Away from the Vatican I tried to live a pious and respectable life with my final husband, Alfonso D'Este.

Alfonso was kind, though always unfaithful. It didn't worry me. As his duchess, I had gained social acceptance and the respectability that I had never thought I would achieve, as the scandal from my first marriage had always seemed to follow me. This of course was aided by Caesare's presence and his drunken rants about the lust he had for me to seemingly close friends. So the rumours about us never fully died. People remembered our escapades, my shocking urge to dress as a boy, and stories and gossip were exaggerated way beyond the truth. It was even attributed to me that I once shot at servants with bow and arrow from a window of the *palazzo*. Of course this was all nonsense. The wild life I'd led had died the day I gave birth to my brother's child.

The collapse of the house of Borgia began the day our father was buried. Scandal once again returned to my household.

Caesare no longer had someone holding him back (although I never knew how Father had managed it). One week after Father's death, my brother's real reign of terror began.

Caesare turned up at my *palazzo* and took my husband out riding one day. Alfonso never entered my bedchamber again. He changed his suite of rooms. Caesare moved into our household and into Alfonso's bedroom, which linked to mine, the next evening.

In a state of confusion I watched the servants bring in his possessions and unpack.

'Why are you here?' I asked Caesare.

'Why, sister. Your dear husband has offered me a home for the time being. He did not want me out on the streets after Father's death.'

'I want you to leave.'

Cold, dark green eyes studied me. 'How uncharitable of you.'

Caesare turned to the servants as they removed his expensive clothing from trunks and hung them in the wardrobes my husband's clothing had once occupied. 'Leave us.'

The servants scurried away. They recognised the violence in him, even more than I did at that time.

'Luci, I thought you'd be pleased to have a real man return to your bed.'

'Is that what you think? That I would let you near me again, Caesare? I hate you and all you stand for. You have debauched your life, escalating the scandal of our family. I have a respectable life with Alfonso and I won't give that up. So, I'm asking you once more to leave here. I won't do as you wish and my door will remain locked to you.'

His eyes were molten rage as he grabbed me, dragging me by the hair across the room. He flung me down in the centre, hit and punched me. Blood burst from my lips, splattering the lampshade by the four-poster bed. I screamed and he fell on me, his blows matched by kisses as he ripped at my bodice. I fought free, raking my nails down his arm. He hit me once more with the back of his hand, sending me crashing back against the bedpost. My head smashed into the frame and I slipped stunned to the floor.

His hands grabbed viciously at my breasts bruising my flesh. There was none of the old tenderness between us. Those days were gone. My brother was not the same. The things we had endured had changed him irrevocably. He held me down, making no attempt to stifle my screams. He knew that no help would come from my husband or the servants. All the gossip I'd heard about his treatment of women was confirmed that night as he ripped my clothing from me and brutally raped me, forcing unwanted kisses on my bleeding lips.

My strength gave out and I lay in a stupor.

'You will never refuse me again,' he told me. 'I am the power now in this household, and your children will suffer unless you please me.'

Despite my screams and cries at his door, Alfonso refused to see me and my attempts to gain his help only resulted in further and more violent beatings. I knew that Alfonso was afraid too, though I did not know why or what had occurred between him and Caesare on that ride. This fear was so elevated that I knew Caesare would make good any threats he had made. Though I screamed and called for help night after night, no one came to my rescue.

Caesare dismissed the nursery staff and brought in his own loyal servants. I was a mother and I feared for my children. So, battered, bruised and afraid, I learnt to please him. I learnt to be his whore whenever and however he wanted and the cruelty of his sex games began. Even so, I adapted. I survived. That's what women do in these circumstances.

'Get the robe off,' he ordered one night after staggering in drunk.

I hated him, but did as he said and I lay on my bed as he took me.

'Kiss me.'

Even though I complied he beat me because I hadn't kissed him like I meant it.

'Tell me you love me,' he slurred. I willingly accepted the blows. No amount of torture could make me say those words to him. I hated him so much.

It wasn't long before I fell pregnant with my final child. Needless to say, the baby was not my husband's. At first Caesare was angry, a pregnancy might spoil his pleasure,; but as the months wore on, he softened a little to me. The beatings stopped. He gave instructions for the servants to ensure I ate properly at all times.

'Why do you care?' I asked once, risking his wrath.

'It's my child in there. Don't delude yourself that I'm being kind to you for your sake.' He sneered. 'I'm thinking only of my child.'

His possessive interest in the baby frightened me. As my belly grew, sometimes he lay in bed with his head resting on me feeling the movement of the child inside. He made me lie naked as he gazed in wonder at my stomach as it twitched. Often in the night he curled up beside me and slept, a contented expression curling his lips. The contempt and rage disappeared from his face. I was reminded of our teenage years and the love that I had briefly experienced with him.

'Pregnancy softens you,' Caesare commented. 'You have been more loving towards me. More genuine in your affection.'

It appeared to be true. It was easier to pretend when he was kind. But I dreaded the birth; I feared the return of the violent side of his nature.

During the final days of my confinement, Caesare, now certain of his ultimate control over us, left to go to Rome on business. The household had not been free of him for almost a year. It was a huge relief. Even the servants changed. Within an hour of him leaving I acted. Calling my loyal servants to me I made immediate arrangements for the removal of my children. I feared for them constantly and reasoned that the new baby might be a little safer as Caesare was, at least, the father. His behaviour so far made me believe there was a chance that he would be a good father to it.

Finally Alfonso helped. He too had been biding his time. He took the children away to stay with a distant relative. I did not even know where they were. But I felt this was for the best; Caesare couldn't beat it from me then. If I promised to stay with him, be his mistress, give him all that he wanted, then surely he would not feel the need to go after my children.

'I'm sorry,' Alfonso said as I stood beside the carriage. 'I betrayed you. I've been such a coward. But I'll be back with the right kind of help, once the children are safe.'

'I know. Caesare is intimidating. Alfonso, please tell me. What did he do to you?'

Alfonso flushed, hung his head. It was so bad that my husband could not even bring himself to say. I reached out, lifted his chin and looked into his shame-filled eyes.

'He did to you what men do to women sometimes,' I said.

Alfonso's eyes filled with tears as he nodded. 'And he threatened to do the same to our children.'

'Oh my God!'

I fell silent. It was bad enough to realise that my brother had raped my husband, but the thought that he had threatened the same for our children turned my stomach. A shooting pain rushed up through my body and my belly spasmed.

'Why not come with us?' Alfonso begged.

'Because he will definitely hunt me down. This ends here. Besides, the pains have started. The baby is on the way.'

Alfonso hugged me. I pushed him away, into the carriage and watched with streaming eyes as it drove away. A terrible fear clutched at my heart; a premonition that this was the last time I would ever see my children. My handmaid, Lena, rushed forward to help me back into the house as the cramps doubled me up.

Halfway to the door a thumping pain shot through my groin, bringing me to my knees. My waters broke, flooding liquid down over my legs. My skirt, sodden, tangled around my ankles and feet and I found it impossible to stand. Lena called for help and two footmen rushed forward to lift me. They carried me, crying and screaming, inside and to my room.

Isabella Maria D'Este was born, yelling into the world on the fourteenth of June. In the absence of my other children I looked at this perfect, beautiful child, with her fluff of black hair, knowing she was my last. Like my first, she was born of incest. I loved her. I sent away the wet nurse, fed her from my own breast; unlike any child I had previously had.

'*Senora*,' the nurse said. 'It's just not done. It's not dignified for a lady in your position.'

'I've often wondered how peasant children can be so robust,' I said to the nurse. 'Surely a mother's milk is the best for her child?'

The nurse didn't know how to reply. She turned away as I uncovered my breast and placed it against Isabella's small mouth. She floundered for a while opening and closing her lips with an almost audible smacking sound. Soon she was suckling. The sensation was both strange and soothing for me. The pain I'd experienced in ridding myself of milk after previous births was immediately relieved as my child fed.

This is natural, I thought. This is how it should be. So, I had learnt something, finally: The value of my children. I had loved the others but not like this, not with this same intensity. Isabella must survive, must grow strong. Must have a better life than I had. With these revelations came the realisation that I didn't want her life ruled by the evil legacy of my family. I didn't want her at the mercy of my brother.

'Nurse,' I called and the woman came to me. 'Help me.'

'Of course, Duchess. What do you need?'

'Take Isabella and leave.'

'Duchess?'

'Take her to the others. My husband will care for her now.'

'I don't understand.' The nurse lifted the baby from my breast and Isabella howled in protest. 'Besides, your husband's location is a secret.'

'There is one here who knows, so he may convey news.' I gave the nurse a huge purse. 'Go to see Abenito, the groom. He'll take you to my husband. Hurry. Caesare will be back any day now. I'm afraid for her.'

The nurse nodded. 'I'm afraid for you when he learns the children have gone. Especially this one.'

'He won't kill me.'

When Caesare returned ten days after her birth, Isabella was safely removed and I was ready to defend her life with all the strength I had left in me.

Even if I died in the process.

Rebirth

Smoke from the candles sent trails up into the air, giving substance to the almost tangible force of power as the circle closed. I lay in the centre. I learnt later that the circle was supposed to provide protection. I never knew what Caesare was protecting himself from.

'It's a game,' he said.

And I always played his games, even though they often repulsed me. But this one was different. He'd carved a symbol into the floor, a five pointed star. It was cut deep into the wood panels, grooved at least an inch wide. Caesare had spent a whole day alone with a set of carpenter's chisels to achieve this, time that I was relieved he was not with me. At each point of the pattern a metal ring was embedded into the floor.

'A pentagram,' he told me as though I should know.

The word and the shape meant nothing to me. He spread my naked body within it, tying my hands and ankles to the rings. The thin rope bit into my wrists with burning intensity and the rough scarred wood under my back dug splinters into my soft white flesh. I was afraid, but didn't object. Instead I forced my face to remain still and impassive with every rough pull and chafe even though my body tensed and winced in protest.

I was expecting punishment for my crime of sending the children away. So far he had said nothing. He barely seemed to notice their absence, but he did ask me about the unborn baby.

'A girl. It was stillborn,' I said.

He grew strangely quiet at this information. His mouth drew into a sharp, stern line.

69

'I see.'

He tightened the ropes further and I couldn't hold back a small whimper.

'I've found a way to keep us together beyond death.'

The mask of my face broke for a second. Terror lurched up from my heart to my throat and I could taste bile. *What insanity was this?*

'Brother,' I cajoled, 'come ... love me. That's what you want, isn't it?'

My seductive voice failed to move him as he stood looking down at me. His eyes studied my blonde curls as they spilled over the straight lines of his hewn pentagram. He knelt again, lifting my head roughly as he pushed the stray hairs back and away, towards the nape of my neck. My hair felt like a velvet pillow but it tilted my head up at an unnatural angle. I watched as he stood, looking once more around my head. I realised he was ensuring that the lines of the pentagram were free from obstruction.

Satisfied, he turned and stepped from the circle, backing away. His eyes gleamed as though on fire. I saw the excitement he was feeling in the quiver of his hands as he turned to his makeshift altar, a small wooden trunk covered in a red satin cloth. Glinting metal pieces were spread between a pair of black candles, which stood in two ornate gold holders he'd taken from the family chapel.

I shivered, but not from the cold. Something akin to arousal rippled through me as he slowly removed his robe. His naked body pleased me; it always had. I licked my lips.

Maybe if I show I am willing? Maybe then he won't hurt me so much.

I was tired of the pain he inflicted, tired of the torture, all in the name of his love for me. I was still weak from the birth of Isabella.

My attention was drawn to his erect penis as he turned to me. The least of it all was the rape. That happened frequently enough for it not to hurt anymore. If you are constantly in a state of terror then fear becomes the norm. Caesare played at pagan rituals. He played at rousing Satan. This was just one more role-play to survive.

I didn't see the dagger until it was too late.

He slashed down at my wrist. Sharp hot pain drew a gasp from my lips and my eyes glazed with shock. I lay numb, scared, as he slashed my other wrist.

'Whaa ...'

'Don't be afraid,' his eyes were fierce now. Something feral lurked there, something I hadn't noticed until now.

My body trembled. Tears leaked through my tightly shut eyelids. Incoherent words poured from his lips as I felt my blood trickle slowly into the deep curves in the wood. The knife slashed again at my ankle, deep but not life threatening. I tried to scream but my mouth, throat and tongue wouldn't work.

The grooves filled with my blood as he chanted and I felt a strange surge of energy as though the pentagram circle was somehow channelling it. I was floating above myself looking down on my outstretched body, watching the blood seep from my limbs in a parody of the crucifixion. This was no Christian rite and certainly no Christian home despite outward appearances.

The candle smoke turned red as the blood seeped around my head. Or did I imagine that change? Perhaps blood had leaked into my eyes. The air shuddered and fear soaked me with perspiration as I collapsed back into myself, once again fully aware of the pain in my body. My limbs throbbed dully. My neck hurt from the forced, uncomfortable position and I tried to turn it.

Caesare's voice, still chanting obscenities, boomed into my throbbing head in time with the steady pulse of my life's blood. He lowered himself down, lying between my legs and took me. No thought or consideration to anything but his own pleasure. The fear had evaporated with my will. He wouldn't let me die; he enjoyed hurting me too much.

Let him play this game out and then tomorrow we will be the picture of propriety at the Sunday service.

'My darling sister. I said you could never escape me.'

My vision seemed dull as I opened my eyes to look at him. I'd heard this so many times, believed it. I would never be free of him, unless … His parted lips frightened me, though I couldn't tell why. My eyes were too blurred. I blinked. Yes. I was sure now. He was different. His teeth glistened in the light and I saw that his canine teeth were extended, longer than usual, and that they tapered to long sharp points. They horrified me even more than the dagger he'd used to spill my blood.

He began kissing my neck with a strange tenderness I hadn't experienced since the days when I had been his willing lover. His lips sucked at my throat drawing strange gasping noises from my lips. Even in this situation his touch was exciting. Nausea clenched my stomach pushing away the fleeting feeling of arousal. In some deep intellectual recess I knew that I was slowly bleeding to death. But I quashed the thought as quickly as it surfaced because I didn't want to fear it anymore. Death would be a welcome respite. Death would be freedom.

'I made a pact,' my brother whispered against my throat; his voice was distorted as my senses dulled. 'I can make you one with me. You'll pleasure me forever, sister. How would that suit you?'

The sickness intensified. The horror of 'forever': my greatest fear realised. It wasn't possible. He was insane, wasn't he? He lifted above me. His hands had rested in the blood pooled at my wrists and he licked it off his fingers. And his teeth! They reminded me of the sharp points I had seen in the mouth of an ancient tiger brought to Rome by a visiting Mongol king.

It's a game. Just a game. As Caesare's sharp, pointed teeth plunged into my throat he continued to ravish me. I knew without doubt that he had never said anything truer. Forever existed, forever was real. Forever was prison in the arms of my abusive, cruel brother.

As I slipped once more into the black abyss of nothingness the idea of 'death' was a fervent prayer, a dream, an unattainable fantasy that would end all my suffering and give me the peace I deserved.

Chapter 14 - Lucrezia's Story
Death Of An Innocent

When I awoke I was back in my bed. The house was eerily quiet and I lay immobile, afraid to move. It was mid-morning. The light shone through the corner of my velvet drapes and as always my maid-servant, Lena, would not enter until summoned. Every morning she was afraid of what state she might find me in. I contemplated ringing the bell to call her but thought it best to examine myself first. It was an odd standard to have when I knew that all the servants were aware of exactly what had been happening to me at the hands of my brother. I had my pride, even when brought so low. I didn't wish to see the pitying gaze in Lena's eyes today. I didn't wish to imagine the gossip that would occur later in the kitchen.

I stretched in bed, testing my muscles gingerly. I expected pain but felt nothing but the satisfaction of the stretch. Before Caesare's return I had been recuperating from Isabella's birth. Now I felt intensely fit and strong again. Curious. I stood, expecting to be overcome with nausea brought on by the blood loss of the previous night. I felt well. The postnatal bleeding which had plagued me since the birth had also stopped. I glanced down at my naked body, expecting to see scabs and bruises. I examined my wrists, and saw to my astonishment no sign of the cuts that Caesare had inflicted on me. They had healed. No matter how closely I looked I couldn't see even the slightest mark to indicate that they had been slashed. I felt better than I had in years.

I began to think that maybe Caesare's return had been a dream. I had been ill and feverish after the birth. It could have been some sort of crazy hallucination. Now I was well again and my fever broken. I breathed a sigh of relief and shuddering slightly, more from the memory of my nightmare than from the coolness of my chamber. As I crossed the room, I reached for my robe and pulled it on around my body, lifting my hair and dropping it down over the collar.

I bent my head from side to side, stretched out my arms and legs, testing my limbs still further. I felt different, renewed. I caught sight of myself in the full-length dressing mirror and froze. My expression was a parody of exaggerated shock. Following the birth of my daughter I'd been weak and gaunt. The stress of a difficult birth and the months of abuse at my brother's hands had left me emaciated and aged. But my cheekbones now held the full bloom of a woman years younger. My body had been changed and marked by pregnancy and yet I gazed down to discover a now flat belly showing through the open robe. All the stretch marks and sagging flesh had disappeared. My waist was small and tight, my breasts once again firm and pert. I fell to my knees.

Sorcery. My hands flew to my mouth, stifling the scream that threatened to spill out. It couldn't be true. It was impossible. I had finally lost my mind! Yet, as I let my hands drop, the full ripe lips that pouted back at me from the polished glass proved I was sane. I had been regenerated in some way. I was transformed. My eyes had been hazel, and now they were intensely green. My fair hair was now a whiter, more silver blonde. The curl that had become lank and thin with age and childbirth was now buoyant and full. My fingertips touched my face, following all its natural curves, confirming that the wrinkles around my eyes had disappeared along with the frown lines from my brow.

I needed to think. It hadn't been a dream after all. Caesare had performed some kind of magical ritual. I looked around the room. *Where was he now?* I checked Caesare's room but it was empty. His trunks lay open ready to be unpacked by the servants. He was here, somewhere.

'Oh my God!' I crouched on the floor and wrapped my arms around my legs, rocking back and forth

He would continue his control of me. Everything he had said came rushing back. Blood coloured my cheeks as panic surged into my head. My breath huffed and I gasped in mouthfuls of air, clawing at my throat in a subconscious reaction to suffocation.

'Forever...'

Caesare's whispered promise echoed in my head along with the memory of his frenzied rutting.

His gasping orgasm poured into me, as his words permeated my brain; which both possessed and stole a little more of my soul.

'Oh my God. Oh no.' I sobbed into my hands.

It was all true.

I staggered to my feet crying so hard I could barely see. I stumbled over to the dressing table, my blind fingers searching frantically. A jar of cream fell from the dresser and thudded to the floor. My fingers brushed a bottle of perfume, tipped it over, sending wafts of flowery scent up into the air. Then my fingers found the knife. Its sharp point pierced the tip of my finger. I ignored the momentary pain. I gripped the handle.

'I wish I was dead ...'

It had to end. My death would help my children; what further claim could Caesare have on them thereafter? My death would absolve my husband of all guilt. My death would be the rightful ending to the sins I had committed. I had started this. It was my fault. After all I had once been willing in my carnal love for my own brother. Only I could finish it.

'Forgive me, Father, for I have sinned ...'

I slashed down on my wrist. I felt the knife slice me, saw the blood well up and pour down my arms. I took the knife weakly in my other hand, and sawed at my other wrist. The knife was sharp and it cut through my fine flesh with little effort. My arm burned, I cried with the pain. Then because of shock, or maybe because my mind just couldn't take anymore, I slipped into blessed blackness. I like to think that a smile curved across my lips as I slumped to the floor.

At last I will know peace.

'Lady. Oh my dearest lady,' Lena stroked the back of my hand. 'Please wake.'

My eyes fluttered open to see my handmaid. She sponged my face with a cool damp cloth. Her dark brown eyes were wide with fear as she soothed my brow.

'What happened?' I asked.

'I don't know. There was a lot of blood on the carpet, but you seem uninjured. You seem ...'

I lifted my arm. The wounds were gone. My heart pounded in terror; my chest heaving painfully. I closed my eyes and shut out the world once more.

I roused slowly. A new calm flowed through my limbs. I felt relaxed, refreshed and strong, as though I'd had a long and restful sleep. Lena held my hand now. I watched her concerned expression change to wonder as I met her gaze. She scrutinised my face.

'Duchess. You look wonderful.'

Lena helped me stand, but I didn't feel weak, just shaken.

'I'm alive ...'

'Yes of course, Duchess.'

I glanced down at the carpet and saw the blood just as the coppery smell hit me. I staggered against Lena. She led me to the bed, throwing back the covers. Pains wracked my stomach. I felt the nausea of intense hunger, a feeling I had rarely experienced. The smell that filled the room, that soft metallic, salty odour, was the most desirable aroma I had ever experienced.

'I feel ... hungry.'

'I'll get you something. Please rest though, Duchess.'

'It hurts!'

I tried to stand, but Lena's kind hands guided me back onto the bed. She swabbed my face once more. She thought I was feverish. The pains rolled through my body and I caught her hand in irritation. I pulled her closer with one small, very strong, movement. Her eyes widened.

Under her skin I felt the ripple and beat of a ruby river. I looked at her skin. I could almost see the flow of blood through her blue veins. I breathed in; she smelt so good. There was an enticing odour around her. I rubbed my face against her arm, listened to the beat; a steady drumming that sped up at my touch. Instinct drove me. I bit her wrist.

Blood gushed into my mouth. The ecstasy was orgasmic. Food, addiction, sexual attraction. Lena swooned in my arms as though I was her lover. I felt strong and invigorated. I pulled her lips to me, kissed her, leaving traces of blood all over her mouth; then trailed it down to her throat. I kissed her neck, suckling the vein that throbbed beneath her porcelain skin. Licked it. The veins under her skin shifted and swelled, as though the blood was drawn up to my mouth. She groaned in my arms. I turned her, pulled her over my body and reversed our positions. She lay beneath me on the bed as I nuzzled her neck and showered kisses all over her face and throat. I was the seducer, not the seduced. For the first time in my life I felt the supremacy of the sexual aggressor. I wanted her. It was eroticism. It was hunger. It was power. And she moaned, thrashing beneath me. Hands clawing at the sheets as I kissed her. Two sharp needle-point teeth now protruded over my lip. I had my own phalluses. My gums ached and throbbed as my fangs extended further. Growing, hardening, like a male member.

I bit her throat, her blood poured as though it was her female moisture. She gasped. I stroked and explored her body. Squeezing her tiny breasts through the fabric of her clothing, which I ripped away to reveal her innocent buds. I lapped at her blood, drinking and sucking greedily, while pinching her nipples. She writhed against me, crying out with pleasure. I wanted to take her like a man. I did in a fashion. I rubbed between her legs as I bit deeper. Her hips rocked against my hand as I let my fingers slide over her virgin mound. Her cries echoed around the room. I didn't care if we were heard. My fangs slid deeper. I fought the urge to plunge them in and out of her like some sort of rapist.

Her blood came faster. With it, my arms tightened and strengthened while my fingers continued to massage her until she screamed my name. My hair covered her face like a shroud, muffling her orgasm. She choked as though even my locks would ingest her. Still she came, over and over until all of her strength evaporated. Lena, an innocent, sweet girl, died during her final orgasm. I drank, taking all of her wonderful liquid down into my stomach where the muscles grew taut as my immortal body fortified.

When no more blood came, I flopped on the bed at her side licking the last clotting dregs from my lips. I felt sated and drifted into the dreamless sleep of the innocent.

Revenant

'Murder!'

I sat bolt upright in the bed to see a young servant girl standing in the open doorway of my room. Her hand flew to her mouth as she stared at me. I stared back at her.

'Murder!' she screamed again, yet her mouth did not move. She was paralysed with fear; somehow I was hearing her terror in her frightened mind.

I shifted position and she let out an ear-piercing scream. She had perhaps thought me dead. I must have seemed like a corpse rising from a satin coffin. A male valet, a scullery maid and a groom entered the room at high speed. All three halted just inside. I gazed back at them in confusion. Their expressions were all the same; each frozen with their mouth open, eyes wide. It was as if time slowed and stopped. They too had expected to find me dead. Instead, I was very much alive. I followed their eyes, turning to Lena as she lay beside me. I gasped.

Lena's throat was gnawed and bloody. It looked as though a wild dog had attacked her. For a moment I was immobile with fear and then I threw myself off the bed, landing crouched on the floor. My robe was half open revealing my breasts. I barely noticed. I shivered, terrified, on the floor beside the bed as more servants bustled into the room. Then the memory of killing Lena flooded my mind.

By now the daylight was slipping into early evening. The housekeeper would have insisted that someone came to check on me, to bring me food, even though I hadn't called. It explained the unexpected intrusion of the young servant girl, who now sobbed against the chest of a robust valet. My movement did nothing to break the paralysis; the servants remained quiet. Their gaping mouths silently cried accusations. I stood, straightened my robe and stared back at them arrogantly. The strength of my vampiric transformation empowered me.

One footman gasped as he arrived, pushing through the others to look into the room. 'Oh my God. He musta killed her and she's come back as a revenant.' His entry broke the silence.

'Take her! She's a monster,' someone shouted.

Instinct and self-preservation kicked in. I ran towards the window, threw open the drapes, and hurled myself through the glass. The sounds of shouts and yells followed me as I fell down three storeys into the garden, landing on all fours as broken glass cascaded around me. The jar of the fall made my bones twinge. My knee was cut and bled briefly, but I was up on my feet and running within seconds. I felt the now more familiar itch of my skin repairing itself. By the time I reached the end of the garden my cuts and scrapes were already healed.

I ran as though hounded by demons. Behind me I could hear the cries of my servants as they rushed down the stairs and out into the garden. They were afraid. I could smell it on the night air. I glanced behind me, could see the flare of torches as they scurried out across the field. But I was entering another stretch of land and they were miles behind.

What witchery had Caesare raised to alter me so much? My mind flicked back to the weird symbol Caesare had cut into the floor. A 'pentagram' he called it. The image nagged at my brain. I'd seen it before somewhere, perhaps a book in the library at St Peter's.

I gathered speed, never tiring, running and running across fields, over hedges and paths. Before long I reached the highway and heard a carriage approaching. I dipped behind the trees lining the road, never slowing, keeping my pace with the carriage. I realised that I could run even faster. The speed was exhilarating. I felt the most intense sense of freedom. I rushed on, loving the whip and pull of the wind in my hair as I hurtled forward. For a time it wiped the fear of my pursuit from my mind. I felt intoxicated by my new strength; it poured into my limber muscles and I hurried on, basking in the thrill of my supernatural speed.

Eventually I crashed through some woods, cutting away from the highway and came to a halt in the middle of a small clearing. My breathing was even. I should be gasping, should be weary, but neither my limbs nor my lungs suffered any ill effects.

The exhilaration seeped away. Terror rushed back into my mind as I remembered my situation. I fell to the leaf-strewn earth.

'I'm dead. A revenant. Just like the servant said.'

I had killed Lena and had enjoyed it. I was dangerous. I lolled on the soft matted ground recalling the sensation of loving her, of feeding on her. My eyes half closed with the memory of the pleasure it gave me. I felt powerful, aroused by her sex and her blood. The guilt resurfaced and my body began to tremble. My mind was as confused as my contrary emotions.

I wrapped my arms around my body and cried. I sobbed for the loss of Lena's life, for my children, for my husband and for my former life. The salty fluid flowed down my cheeks unchecked. My ribs heaved and sighed until they ached.

For a long time after the tears subsided I lay listless. I felt the twitch and tickle of insects as they crawled over my still body. The cool leaves and moss beneath me was a comfort to my fevered flesh. The ants and beetles seemed a fitting blanket for my abnormal carcass.

'Ashes to ashes, dust to dust...'

I'm dead, I thought. Worms should feed on me. This is a suitable end.

The beguiling five-pointed symbol burned once more in my mind, imprinting itself on my brain. It danced seductively behind my eyes.

'Pentagram.'

Freedom

A sweet, dusty scent awoke me, mingled with the smell of food being cooked on an open fire. It was newly dawn. The sky was vaguely pink, but already I could feel the prickle of the sun's heat seeping through the trees. I sat up, blinked, and gazed at my surroundings. I wasn't sure for a moment how I had come to be here and then the memories of the last two days came flooding back. I sank back against the nearest oak, as if the solidity of the ancient wood could steady me. If I was dead, and I didn't think I was actually dead, then how did I have awareness? Do the dead weep? Do the dead sleep and then re-awake?

I looked down at my hands; grime and dirt covered my skin. I looked like I'd crawled from a grave. When I shook my arm the dirt fell away leaving my skin completely smooth and clean. Curious.

I stood, scrutinising the muscle tone in my leg as I pushed aside the filthy robe to reveal my bare skin. My body had evolved still further. It must have been the blood I drank. I'd thought I had imagined feeling my muscles harden as I had sucked the life from Lena. The memory of kissing her, of touching her intimately, brought a flush to my face. The thought of murdering her – eating her life-force – was simultaneously the worst and the best memory. Guilt churned my stomach and I slid once more to my knees.

Ants swarmed around me. My vision inexplicably zoomed in. I scrutinised the tiny antennae of one insect as it reached out to smell me. A multitude of eyes within bulbous black eyes watched me, were alert to my interest, as it twitched nervously. It seemed

83

to have its own set of fangs, but in many ways its mouth reminded me of the pincers of a lobster. It had six spindly, yet powerful, legs and a large bee-like back end. With a jolt, I realised that usually these features were invisible to the naked eye. I had never really analysed anything in nature before. As I turned my gaze away I felt the ant, heard it even, scurry after its sisters in their search for food. I fell once more into a trance-like stupor as I examined the grass and mud, and the multitude of living things that squirmed and crawled there. The insect world was a fascinating place.

A chopping sound nearby roused me. A woodcutter was working the woods; the smell of food was clearly his. I stood up and slid away deeper into the forest. It was essential that I remained unseen. I weaved in and around oaks until the trees thinned once more.

Smoke poured from the chimney of a small cottage. I heard the noises of farm animals in a pen around the back; the snort of a pig, the clucking and screeching of hens and the crow of the cockerel as he proclaimed the dawn.

The morning opened up fully and the sun's intensity made my exposed arms itch as if a thousand insects were climbing all over my skin. I swatted my flesh, believing the feeling to be the ants I'd seen. There was nothing there. I felt sick and dizzy. I slithered back into shade. Both the nausea and the itching stopped. I experimented by raising one arm and stretching it out of the shade into the light. The sensation returned so I yanked my arm back to gain immediate relief. The sun was a source of discomfort for me when openly exposed to it.

A young girl came out of the cottage dressed in a coarse blue dress. I squatted down among the foliage. A grubby apron was tied around her waist and she carried a bucket of grain on her hip.

'Druda!' yelled a voice from within the cottage.

'*Si, Madre?*'

'Don't forget to collect the hens' eggs too.'

Druda tutted. Her brown hair was unkempt and unwashed but she had a pretty face. '*Si, Madre.*'

'And then take the washing down to the river ...'

Druda stopped, turned and looked back at the cottage.

'I'm a slave in this house.' The girl sighed, and then singing softly with good nature, she went around the back of the cottage. I heard the soft patter of grain falling at the feet of hungry birds.

I moved around the back of the house. Druda sloshed swill into the pigs' trough. There were three pigs. They dived over each other, shoving one another aside as they guzzled the foul smelling waste into their greedy mouths. Within minutes the trough was empty and the pigs squealed in protest. Their gobbling mouths opened and closed as they pushed against the wood. Druda watched them for a moment before moving to the hen house where she began gathering eggs, placing them gently into the bucket she had used to fill the trough.

I remained hidden, watching the girl work and listening to her mother shout orders from inside the cottage. After washing clothing in the river Druda returned to the yard and proceeded to peg up undergarments and another coarse woollen dress onto a line that was strung between a couple of trees. She went inside the cottage where I heard her spoon out some broth for her ailing mother. The women barely talked. I could hear the rustle of bread being torn and the soft slap of spoons dipping quickly in and out of their bowls as they gulped the food down.

It was an odd experience. Sitting on the outskirts of such humble life, knowing I was now no longer part of the living world. Could I ever be in it again? I became aware of my dress and the disadvantage of only having my robe. For the first time I considered going home to collect some things, but knew this was impossible. A militia would be waiting for me, of that I was certain. Then there was Caesare. My mind stumbled again. Confusion at my altered state led me to wonder if my brother too possessed the same strength and speed that I did. I remembered all too well how his teeth had grown into catlike fangs as mine had. The changes wrought were definitely down to him. A new horror gripped me. He knew I'd change, become the same as him, and he could keep me; torture me, for all eternity. Because how can the dead die?

My mind was blank as I watched like a voyeur as Druda left the cottage once more and continued with her chores. How simple and uncomplicated her life seemed compared to mine. Filled with wealth and privilege, my world had for the most part been a silent hell. I'd have given anything in that moment to be this girl. To take over her life and live it in comparative freedom. The thought idled in my brain briefly. But no, this was still too close to my home. It would be so easy for Caesare to find me.

A candle flame burned in the back of my brain, igniting the realisation that I now had an abundance of freedom. Caesare may have only just learned of my flight. He was the only person who could possibly find me. I leapt to my feet as Druda left the yard on her way once more to the river. Rushing forward I yanked the damp clothing from the line and ran.

Deep into the forest I stopped once more to clothe myself, wrapping a shawl around my head to hide the abundance of beautiful hair that shone over my shoulders. I dirtied my hands and face again. I looked down at my discarded robe. I had to destroy it, or at least bury it. It would be too obvious a clue to my brother who had hunted all his life. Looking around I could see no obvious place to dispose of the garment so I rolled it up and tucked it carefully under my arm. The silk was so dirty and stained now that it looked like nothing more that some peasant rag. Finally satisfied, I stepped out onto the road, like a harmless peasant travelling to market.

After walking briskly for a mile or two I observed the emptiness of the road and gathered speed, running full pelt towards the next small village. Here I would move among the peasants to see if any rumours had spread of Lena's murder. I realised that I had now put many miles between my home and myself. It was unlikely that anyone would be looking for me this far away.

However, Caesare's name floated through my head. My brother had gone to extreme lengths to own me. I had to remain alert. After all I didn't know what he was capable of.

Having run the last ten miles on the darkening road, weaving in and out of the trees as the road traffic thickened, I reached the outskirts of the town at nightfall. It was a place called Tramonti. I knew by some bizarre new instinct that I was south of Rome. It was a small village with very little to offer other than a tiny community.

I entered under cover of darkness. It was evident that it would be impossible for me to remain anonymous here. The town was too small and the villagers all knew each other well. It was obvious that my presence would attract too much attention so I quickly hid myself in the shadows, listening at doorways.

'My cousin doesn't make up stories, Tita.'

The peasant's loud voice echoed through the open shutter and I was drawn to the hatch to listen.

'You come from the tavern and you tell me tall tales told to children to make them behave! Your cousin drinks too much and has too vivid an imagination.'

'No, no. I tell you ...'

'Yes, you tell me a monster roams and eats young girls. There are many monsters in this world but certainly it is not a Duchess turned into a revenant. Go to bed, Ernesto. I will not listen to this drunken nonsense any more this evening.'

Even this far, news of Lena's murder was filtering through. I knew I had to leave immediately, move onto another town still further away. But ultimately I needed to lose myself in the bigger cities. An image of the Vatican flared up behind my eyes like a welcoming beacon. Rome. I felt the pull of my past dragging me along and through the village. I followed the glow in my mind like a well-learned map. I was going home. Somehow I knew the way.

The Hunt

The road is dark, an A road with no streetlights. This is never a problem for me as I have perfect night vision. Lilly strokes my leg. I am driving for once. She has given up insisting that she is more capable than I. We are looking for a hotel, something quiet and remote, away from the city. I need somewhere quiet to think and to try and make sense of the stories that Lucrezia has been telling me.

'Do you know anywhere in the area?' I ask Lilly.

'Just drive. There are hundreds around here.'

I feel the swirl of energy a few seconds before something lands in the road before us. Excellent reflexes help me brake in time. I sit for a moment looking at the humped figure, knowing it is a body lying at an unnatural angle. It is crumpled in the road directly in the beam of my headlights. Lilly jumps from the car and rushes to examine it before I can prevent her and so I too am forced to leave the car. I feel uneasy.

The man is of some vague mixed race. His head and face are crushed from the fall, body twisted and bent. One arm is pulled up over his head, the hand crushed and warped around the wrong way. That's how I see the tattoo, or I might never have recognised him. It is a Celtic fish on a hook. The victim is the waiter from the bar the other night and I recall that I had fleetingly considered killing him for his attitude.

'Same as our friend Ellie, except ...' Lilly hands me a piece of paper as I stand looking down at the mangled remains. It is a note, written in the victim's blood.

Mother

'What does it mean?' Lilly asks.

'I don't know. The killer has an Oedipus complex?'

I take the note with us and throw it into the back of the car. I can sense the aura of the entity ... alien, different.

We follow the entity's trail for almost an hour, all the time staying well back. It leaves a black essence, like a threatening calling card, along the road. We can sense it, taste it, smell it, even though it is invisible to the naked eye. It beckons us. I am unable to resist the call, although Lilly is a little more cautious.

'It's human in shape. Male,' Lilly says. I don't know how she can tell: I can barely make out its outline on the horizon.

I turn the car into an unlit lane. We are somewhere in Cheshire. I watch the headlights bounce as we make our way along the uneven track. Ahead of us, the creature has changed its direction. It halts in the air and comes flying back towards us. I react by braking hard. The car skids in the mud, with its huge wheels scraping noisily against a raised, natural grass verge on the driver's side, before coming to a halt. The being, *He*, draws closer.

Lilly digs her nails in my arm. I feel the blood seeping from my torn skin as I turn to her. Her face is still and beautiful. She doesn't appear afraid, but I can feel her nervousness as her aura laps mine. She always touches me when she feels worried.

Darkness.

Nausea rips at my insides as vitality leaks from my limbs. My head flops back. I have no control over my body, not even my neck. I feel Lilly slump beside me. Her breathing becomes shallow. My stomach clenches. I feel hollow and worried for her, despite my own pain. Coldness slips into my veins as my blood turns to icy sludge.

Paralysis.

I stare up at the sky through the sunroof. The night is scattered with the worlds of the galaxy. I wait. Reason tells me that if we can sense this *thing* then surely it knew of our presence. We are clearly being stalked.

Nothing happens.

The stars stare down declaring me paranoid. Outside the car, the sounds of nature make a mockery of my phobia even though my body is a prisoner. The haunting call of an owl echoes through the trees on the right. I hear the hopping rustle of a hare, the twitter of insects, the crackle of leaves falling in the breeze. All normal night-time sounds exaggerated by my sensitive hearing.

A black blur gathers around my eyes. I force them to focus on the sunroof. Above me a hole appears in the sky and swallows the stars. It floats high above us, stopping over the car. I can feel it looking.

'Mother!' The cry is mournful. For a moment I imagine it is all in my mind.

Lilly gasps. It is the only sound either of us is capable of making. I try to turn my head but can't move. I concentrate all my efforts into moving my head and I turn it with effort, catching the frozen outline of my lover as she gazes up open-mouthed.

'Mother!' it calls again. The voice is male.

Lilly blinks. She too is forcing her body to work again.

'Old ...' she croaks. I also feel the age of the creature. It makes my skull ache.

I feel eyes boring into me and my head flops back again. Still I can see nothing. My eyes burn. Pressure builds behind them. My brain throbs as though I will suffer some vampiric aneurysm. The pain is excruciating. Small sounds force from my lips. Maybe this is how a diver feels when he goes too deep? My ears hurt. I'm certain the drums will burst if relief doesn't come soon. My eyes and nose stream blood, not water or any other secretion that leaks from them.

'Stop it,' Lilly gasps and immediately the tension behind my eyes releases.

The relief is instant. The muscles in my face and neck cramp; they have been held so taut that they ache.

'Leave us alone,' Lilly shouts at the entity.

I hear the wind rush around it, helping it gather speed as it soars higher, heading – I don't know where – but away. As fast as possible, almost as if obeying her command.

My limbs awake and I throw myself against the door, coughing and spluttering as I pull at the handle. My fingers feel numb, the strength barely returning. The door flies open, tumbling my frantic body outside onto the dirt track road. I land on all-fours, vomiting up the blood and steak we had consumed that evening. The nausea is endless. I dry heave until my stomach, throat and mouth hurt from the effort.

'Gabi,' Lilly croaks.

I crawl around the car, unable to stand. I find Lilly on her knees too. Her stomach balks. I smell the sickness on her breath. Beside her, I hold her hair away from her face until the nausea leaves her. She collapses against me and I hug her close. Afraid, so very afraid that the thing we have encountered could have killed her. She is so young, so much more fragile than I.

When we feel able, I turn the car and head back to Manchester. Hopefully Lucrezia will have some answers soon.

Escape

Rome had not been my home for several years. As I made my way there, travelling by night and sleeping by day, I reflected on the corruption of my life. I missed my children and wondered often if they were safe, especially Isabella. Was my new baby thriving without my love? Since the night of my rebirth there was not even the pain of mother's milk left in my breasts to remind me of my child. I had altered so much, was now completely inhuman. Childbirth could probably never recur in my new and improved body. Even so, I intended to forsake men now. They had been cruel and faithless. My brother's influence felt like a distant nightmare. With every step I took away from my old life, I began to believe I could forget all that had happened.

During the day I felt reasonably strong, even though the sun was excessively painful at times. But in the night I had superior strength. The moon shone on my limbs with glowing energy. In the woods, under cover of dark, I danced like a witch in the glare of the moon, all the time watching my whitening flesh glow luminous. It was as though my skin reflected its cold flame. For to me the moon was cold; I could feel its freezing rays as intently as I could suffer the burning touch of the sun.

I would walk or run through the night. I felt no fear alone, though when I slept in the daytime, I could have been vulnerable. Even then I had no concerns that I could be hurt or that I was in any danger. Maybe it was foolish to allow this feeling of invulnerability to wash through me like a cleansing fire purging a sinner. It wiped away all traces of the pain I'd suffered during my human life. I didn't feel evil, but knew I must be. Therein lay the ultimate freedom. I did not fear death; I was already shunned by God. No man could harm me; I knew I could outmatch the strongest.

The hunger, at times, was agony. I scrambled around for food, drank water from streams; caught fish with my bare hands and cooked them in the woods outside of the towns. No matter how much food I ate, the emptiness and pain was never eased. I stumbled on, sometimes feeling like an addict deprived of some terrible obsession. Through woods and forests, into towns, stealing food whenever and wherever I could. Yet the hunger intensified until it gnawed at my insides. The pain of it threatened to drive me mad.

So, almost insane, feeling every inch an outcast, a revenant, I reached the final village that would mark the last leg of my journey to Rome. It was mid afternoon. I had roused myself early and walked through the burning sun to reach the town before the night watch locked the gates. By now my peasant garb was dirty and I felt invisible amongst the other peasants.

As I walked through the gate I saw her for the first time: An olive-skinned, pretty girl. Clearly from a good family, though not aristocracy. Her dark hair shone with auburn highlights in the afternoon sunshine. Her open, warm eyes were light brown, flecked with hazel. She was slender, girlish and fragile. As I looked at her, stepping up into her carriage beside her mother and younger brother, a strange lust rushed into my loins. I felt my gums prick as my teeth extended. I began to believe that in some way I had changed sex. I had never looked at other women this way, although I had always been able to recognise beauty and charm in others. I stumbled against the wall of a local shop and pushed myself around the corner to avoid being seen. And there I watched her carriage depart. I wanted to follow, had to, but was afraid that I would be seen. I wished right then and there that I could be truly invisible, that I could follow totally unseen.

A cold numbness entered my limbs. I stared down at my body. My clothing and my skin had merged into the wall. I had begun to melt away. I cried out in fright and my body appeared whole again immediately. As I stood there, I thought once more of the subconscious wish I'd made. I had willed myself invisible, and it had happened. Could that be possible? Consciously I desired invisibility again. I watched in amazement as my colours changed, observed how I merged, or seemed to merge, with the scenery even when I moved.

I glanced up at the road, and could no longer see the carriage. I believed at that point I would never see the girl again. I began to move deeper into the town, looking for a place to rest. All thoughts of her pushed away by my new discovery. I walked through the village completely unnoticed now. The coldness in my limbs became more comfortable the more I retained the invisibility. I stood in the middle of a bakery shop, admiring the pastries, cakes and bread; all luxuries I had been denied over the previous weeks. I rested my hand on a loaf. My contact affected its appearance immediately. I soon realised that I could take what I wanted and no one would ever see. The food disappeared at my touch so I helped myself and folded the goods into my clothing before scurrying away. Finding a corner, I sat and ate. The food tasted like nectar. After eating, I went into the stable attached to the tavern and climbed up into the hayloft to sleep.

The next day I woke to the sounds of a stable hand whistling as he fed the only horse stabled there. I heard the horse crunching the hay, smelt the sickly sweet odour of the dried grass mingled with the animal's saliva. The boy left and quickly returned with a bucket of water, which he tipped into a trough. As the animal ate and drank, I watched the boy examine the horse's legs, lifting its hooves as he used a knife to clean out the road grit from its shoes. I wondered how I might slip away unnoticed but then recalled my latest discovery from the previous night.

Invisible, I slipped out of the stables, into the street, ready to examine the shops and houses of the village. Now that I could move about unseen, the need to leave quickly diminished. I was curious about being around people again. I knew I wouldn't starve as taking food and clothing would no longer be difficult.

The streets were still deserted as I walked down them, weaving in and out of the well-structured buildings. This close to Rome, the town was more civilised than the others I'd been in so far; the formations more like Roman houses and roads. It was a large town. It had many amenities, including a bath house; a desirable prospect. The touch of warm water was something I had almost come to believe I would never feel again so I kept it in mind to do later. There was the bakery again, a ladies dressmaker, a general store, a grocer and of course a market that sold fresh fish, meats, imported fabric and all kinds of household items from brooms to pots and pans.

I wandered through the market watching the merchants set up and stood by as the morning extended. The meat stall drew me. The smell of blood pulled at my insides. I knew I needed it, had to have it. But would animal blood fulfil me as much as human? The market began to fill. A servant girl weaved her way through the crowd towards the meat vendor; she had such strange arrogance that she drew my attention. Behind her loitered a young mother and a small child followed closely by the husband. I watched their progress as they travelled from one stall to another. The servant leading, the employers following. Then I saw the exchanged looks between the man and the girl and realised where her haughtiness came from. For now at least, she was the honoured lady of the house, the wife merely a token or figurehead. I turned away as I heard the screams and wails of another child. My eyes fell on a small boy, who I vaguely recognised. He was standing before a stall selling toys. No longer invisible, I merged with the crowd, moving closer to hear the conversation.

'Joanna said I could have it!' the boy cried. 'She promised.'

'I know, Peatro, but your sister isn't here. We must wait. She's gone to see the dressmaker.'

'But I want it now!'

The governess glanced at the stallholder, shrugging with slight embarrassment as Peatro stamped his foot.

'She will be here shortly. I didn't bring my purse with me.'

'Then I'll take it and you wait here for Joanna to pay.'

The stall holder twitched his long moustache nervously, 'I'm sorry but nothing leaves my stall until paid for.'

Peatro looked at the man with contempt. 'Do you know who I am? My father is the justice here.'

The governess sighed. She had obviously seen Peatro play this one out before. 'Peatro …'

'Joanna!' the boy shouted. The pretty girl I'd noticed the day before appeared. 'They won't let me have the gift you promised.'

Joanna patted her brother indulgently and promptly paid for the wooden top that he desired. Peatro snatched it from the stall and ran off down the street to try it out. The governess followed.

'Sorry,' Joanna said to the stall owner. 'He is only a boy, and not very patient.'

The stallholder said nothing, but handed Joanna her change. She quickly walked away, a slight flush of embarrassment colouring her cheeks.

I moved closer to the stall.

'Who is she?' I asked.

I met the man's gaze. For a moment it seemed as though he would send me away without answering. After all I no longer looked like the proud lady I once was. My manner too felt as lowly as my dress. I wore the grime of several weeks on the road. The man rolled his eyes and sighed.

'She is Justice Adimari's eldest daughter, and pleasant enough. The boy is her spoilt little brother.'

'Thank you.'

My eyes followed as Joanna continued to weave through the crowd and away from the small market. Compelled, as I had been when I first saw her, I pursued. Joanna Adimari's simple beauty had completely seduced me.

Obsession

I tracked them home. I had to. My obsession with Joanna pulled me along as though I had been tethered to her with an invisible cord. Her beauty and innocence were my seduction. Her patience, my desire. Her blood, my need.

For part of the journey I had to hide myself from human eyes once more. The streets were empty as we left the town centre, but my fangs burst forth at the distant sight of her. It was an instinctive response to a desire that was both sexual and impulsive. It was completely beyond my control. On some level I recognised it as a crush reminiscent to those I'd had with various men throughout my life. Guilt at the perversity of wanting another woman in this way crept up the back of my neck, where I felt my skin flush and prickle.

Desire drove me. I was its victim. Joanna had me in her thrall. I knew that what I needed from her could only be taken, would never be freely given. I knew that what I wanted would be effectively rape, the same as I had suffered at the hands of my brother for all those years. That thought alone should have sent me scurrying away in shame and horror, but the idea of being the one in control and of taking someone else for my own needs was so compelling that I had to see how far I could go.

Joanna and her family lived in a house next to the court, in the centre of the town. The Justice had accumulated wealth, probably as all of them did, from the handouts of the semi-wealthy merchants who wanted favours from him in return. It was business. Politics. I understood these things too well, had seen them in my own childhood world. Many an innocent would have paid the price for the Justice's political advancement. But with money and power also came enemies, and the Justice's enemies could find him all too easily. Therefore the house was surrounded by a high wall which completely enclosed it, keeping out the criminal world and keeping him and his family safe.

As they approached the house I noticed the discreet guard that flanked their progress along the road. How stupid of me not to observe them weaving in and out of the crowd in the market. Joanna and Peatro ignored the six men; clearly this was borne out of a lifetime of familiarity, but the governess glanced at them nervously as they drew closer to the huge gates of the house. One of the guards whistled, and a side gate swung open allowing them all to enter.

I stood across the street, watching my obsession disappear into the whitewashed building. As the door closed behind her it was as if a magnet had been switched off. My fangs retracted. I was trembling. I felt like the victim.

Rage took me swiftly. Anger and pain, mixed with grief and remorse. I had been in the thrall of someone else, and I hated her for that. I realised that, in my new life, no one should have power over me. I was in control of my life and destiny. I had amazing strength and speed. I would never willingly lose control. Joanna's beauty was a fascination. It had compelled me, but in the end I could, if I wanted, walk away. My mind, not my new nature, would decide.

At that moment, my mind wanted to kill Joanna Adimari.

I waited until night had fallen, growing hungrier by the minute. As soon as it was dark, I crept unheard and unseen into the house of the Justice. It was so easy now I was invisible. I scaled the wall that surrounded the house as though it was nothing. The merest dent or groove was an easy foot or hand-hold for me as I gathered speed and almost flew to the top. Once there I looked down the other side. The drop was around thirty feet into the courtyard. There was a guard below and despite my chameleonic nature I was concerned that I might be hurt from the fall and be caught, so I walked along the top of the wall. It was so easy to balance; I felt like a cat strutting through the night, and, as I'd noticed previously, my night vision was excellent.

Halfway around, the wall passed close to an elaborate bedroom balcony. Candlelight flickered within the room. I paused, looking inside, trying to see whose room this was. It was simply furnished with a plain bed, a dresser, and a wardrobe. After a few moments I noticed the governess moving inside. She blew out the candle and left.

The family were gathering for dinner. I could hear the chatter from the dining room below. The gentle clatter of places being set echoed up through the house. I knew only that my sensitive ears could make out these distant and compelling sounds. They told me a story, almost conveying the image of the act into my mind. I could see the servants rushing around; every movement I heard showed me the image in my mind's eye.

There was one young maid being instructed by the housekeeper.

'Not like that. Like this.' Knives and forks and crystal glasses were placed neatly on the table.

The Justice and his wife were in the lounge, drinking fortified wine. I could smell the alcohol.

'Peatro, don't play with that toy in here ...' *Senora* Adimari said firmly.

'I want to play! I'm bored.' Peatro stamped his foot in what I now knew was a characteristic display of temper.

I zoned out from the argument that ensued, scanning every spoken word for the sound of her voice. But Joanna was not in the room yet. Or else she was sat so quietly that I could not detect her. Then I heard her name.

'You're a lucky man, Marco. There's many in town would give their right arm for a chance to wed Joanna. Not least that she is the Justice's daughter.'

'Yes. I feel lucky.'

I felt sad for Joanna. She was beautiful, and a commodity to these people, just as I had been to my father. I could surely do something to prevent that. My bite would free her, wouldn't it? I could take her with me as a sister, a companion. We could travel the world. Obtaining wealth would be so easy now. I could take all that I wanted, who could stop me? And I would take Joanna.

My thoughts tumbled away again. My obsession with Joanna confused me yet excited me too. Justifying a friendship seemed to help me make sense of it. Then I remembered Lena. She was dead and had not transformed; I had savaged her. Or had I? Maybe Lena had healed and risen again. I hadn't stayed around to find out after all. Somehow I knew she hadn't lived. I knew that Lena lay in a cold dark grave, rotting as every corpse did. Could I bring death again to another innocent?

I hesitated for a moment, surveying the distance between myself and the balcony. My indecision had little to do with fear of falling; I was considering leaving. Then the aroma of Joanna's perfume wafted up to me from the half open dining room window below. I leapt from the wall onto the balcony before I even acknowledged I wanted to.

It was interesting how my body responded to my every thought. I had unlimited agility and speed. I compared my new flexibility to the circus acts I'd seen as a child, who performed gymnastic and aerial combinations with ease. I swung on the canopy above the balcony, leaping up to catch the bar easily. There was no muscle ache, pain or discomfort in any way. I performed several exercises there, lifting my whole body up and down as though I weighed nothing more than a feather.

I heard the family enter the dining room and dropped silently back down onto the balcony. As I suspected, the doors to the room were unlocked. They did not expect anyone to be able to reach this room. Therefore my entry was made simple. Once inside I headed for the hallway and went in search of Joanna's room.

I could sense her now. It was like the trace of perfume I'd smelled earlier, though I knew it was more likely her natural essence. It filled the hallway, and I stood silently breathing her in for a moment. Her odour filled me and made me lose my sense of self once more. She was like opium and I thought that my addiction for her might become the focus of my whole revenant existence. I could almost see her image burning in the trail of scent all down the hallway.

At the top of the stairs the fragrance parted. The strongest trail led downstairs where I knew she must now have joined her family and fiancé. I wanted instead to see her room, so I followed the fainter scent across the upper landing and towards a closed door on the other side of the hallway. Overwhelmed by her essence I opened her door and walked inside. Closing the door behind me, I sighed and leaned my back against the wood. As I relaxed I allowed myself to once again become visible.

Joanna's room was perfectly tidy except for a robe that lay casually across the bed. There was a porcelain tub of bath water cooling before the fire. Clearly the servants had yet to get round to emptying it. I examined the selection of fine powders and pale pink rouge pots on her dressing table. She had a beautiful hand mirror, comb and brush set, all with engraved silver handles. I lifted the brush and caught sight of my dishevelled appearance in the dressing mirror. My hair was a matted mess, my skin crusted with filth. I looked like the crazed revenant my servants had called me. I looked like a monster. Joanna would be terrified of me, and I didn't want her to be afraid.

I stripped away my clothing and slipped into the still-warm bath water, listening carefully for signs of the servants. The water felt wonderful. The things I had taken for granted all of my life were now luxuries I had been denied, or could no longer afford. Picking up Joanna's rose-scented soap I scrubbed the grime from my body and hair, rinsing my scalp by ducking under the water until it felt soap and dirt free. Then I lay there, enjoying the feeling of the water sloshing over my limbs as it grew cold. I closed my eyes, imagining I was in the comfort of my own world once more. An intense homesickness squeezed my heart until I replaced those feelings aside with thoughts and images of Joanna.

Relaxed, I stayed too long. I heard the rapid approach of two servant girls in the hallway. I stood quickly, looking around the room until I saw the towel spread over the back of the chair near the bed. Then I rushed across the room, grabbed the towel and shifted once more into invisibility. As the door opened my eyes fell on my dirty clothing, discarded by the bath. I hurried across the room, scooped up my dirty clothing and pushed it under Joanna's bed seconds before the two girls entered.

One of them halted as she saw the bedspread flop down, while the other babbled happily about the group now dining below us.

'*Signor* Marco is so beautiful. *Signorina* Joanna is going to be so happy.'

'Did you ...?' The first girl, a small waif of about fifteen, pointed to the bed.

'*Si*, it is the wind.'

The first girl shrugged.

'We better empty this and tidy up a little.'

The girls began to empty the water from the bath. Once they had filled two buckets each, the first one opened the balcony windows and they stepped outside to tip the water out onto the streets. I followed them, noticing that Joanna's balcony was almost touching the wall. Good, it would make a better exit.

I moved aside as the girls came back and continued their work. They smelt hot and sweet. My blood rushed to my face as one of them brushed too closely by me. I raised one hand towards her and had to restrain myself from stroking the skin of her neck with my fingers. Their blood called to me.

'It's cold in here,' said the waif. 'Like someone walked over my grave.'

'Strange. The window was closed.'

Once it was empty the girls picked up the bath and carried it away, the four buckets now stored inside it for ease. I could smell the faint aroma of their sweat as they heaved the heavy bath up. I noticed how beautiful the older girl's arms were, defined and toned from the hard work. I'd seen girls like this in my own household; their attractiveness was always short lived. Hard work and marrying young often marred them long before their time.

'Don't you think this house is creepy sometimes?' The waif shuddered as she swung the door wide open with her small foot.

'*Si*. My cousin worked here before she married, she said she heard weird noises in the night.'

I watched their retreat and as the door closed behind them I quickly grabbed Joanna's robe from the bed and pulled it on. Tying the belt loosely I listened at the door. The maid's superstitious chatter receded down the hall and faded as the girls moved deeper into the house.

I felt a little dazed and confused. They'd been aware of my presence even though they couldn't see me. I looked at my arms. The second girl had felt coldness as she passed me. Was that the chill of the dead? I sat on the edge of Joanna's beautiful lace-covered four-poster bed. I felt the cold seeping from my limbs as I faded back to my normal colours again. This magic had to be evil.

I felt colder and emptier now. The hunger began to gnaw inside my stomach as never before. Maybe, by using my power too much, I had drained the energy from myself. I wasn't sure. Suddenly, I felt weak, and lay back, enjoying the sensation of a soft mattress under my back for the first time in weeks. I waited. Waited eagerly for the girl to return. I needed to feed.

Coffee At Harvey Nichols

I stir my *latte* as Lucrezia stares down into her *mocha* as if answers might be found there. I suppose she is thinking that I might be shocked. Her confession, her story, is similar to mine. I hadn't realised how very alike we were. I feel an obscure empathy. Her life has been so terrible; a childhood fraught with danger and abuse. But this is where our lives differ the most, because my childhood was ordinary and loving by comparison. Yet we were both thrown into the world of immortality without the means to resist. Without choice.

'I'm sorry. You had to learn it all alone. Just like me.'

'Perhaps it's the only way,' she shrugs.

I give Lucrezia time to consider whether she will tell me more as a middle-aged waitress begins to clear the table beside us. I watch mesmerised as the woman stacks tea cups and plates noisily onto a tray. Then she extracts a cloth from her pinny and wipes away the spillages of the previous customer.

This is our third meeting. I am beginning to build a strange friendship with Lucrezia that I never thought would be possible. I actually like her, and yet I had spent so many years hating and resenting her intrusion into my life. But there is no love interest now which fortunately will make introducing her to Lilly so much easier. I've decided I must do this anyway. Although I have only scratched the surface of her story, it seems to me that the end of it will be crucial to our continued existence. I have so far resisted telling Lucrezia anything of my suspicions. I don't want my words to change the reflection of her narrative. I want her to be the storyteller as she sees it. And then, well, maybe we will consider the implications together. Strangely, she has not asked me anything more about why I sought her out. But she does question me on occasion about Lilly.

Lucrezia lifts her coffee cup to her red lips and sips her drink. I sip mine in reflection of her.

'So, what have you told her so far?'

'That I'm ready to share the final piece of my past.'

Lucrezia laughs cynically. She knows me too well. It categorically wasn't anywhere near that easy.

Lilly was furious that I wouldn't tell her anything. 'What the fuck are you playing at, Gabi?' she'd asked. But I'd shrugged and smiled, kissing her silent until her questions turned to moans of passion in my arms.

'But she has to trust you while you gather the pieces together?'

'Yes.'

And trust is such a hard thing for a twenty-first century strong-willed female. Telling the past, bringing the subject forward, admitting the truth is even harder for a seventeenth century male. And there never is a good time to tell some stories.

I watch Lilly sleep serenely for over an hour before she wakes. Sitting in the chair beside the bed, I enjoy her slow awareness, the stretch of her limbs, the gentle rubbing of her eyes. She is my creature, my lover, my child, my wife. All her movements, so perfect and beautiful to me, would forever fill me with love and desire. And I do mean 'forever'. Immortality has never been more attractive. My future and happiness all lay in her arms and in her love of me, and fear of losing that kept me quiet longer than it should have.

'What are you doing there?' she asks with a smile.

'Watching you.'

'That could be considered very creepy, you know,' she giggles. 'But I love you watching me.'

'Do you?'

She stretches again, her full breasts poking over the sheets and I lean forward, immediately aroused by her nakedness.

'That's why,' she laughs. 'I love that you desire me so much. Do you think you'll ever stop?'

'Oh my God, no! My emotions aren't fickle, and I don't change my mind so easily. I love you, Lilly.'

'Then come to bed and show me ...'

I stand and begin to move to her like a waking dreamer, or a hypnosis subject, aware but compelled. I smile and stop; it was important not to be distracted. I needed to tell her.

'Soon,' I return to my chair. 'We have to talk.'

'That sounds ominous.'

I sit back, still enjoying the view she is provocatively presenting. Her leg slips out from under the sheet and wraps over and around it. I examine every beautiful toned curve. The sheet has fallen over her shape, her slim waist, her round hips: all call out to distract me further until I close my eyes. Her image is burned on my retinas. Maybe I should relieve us both first? But no, I am merely procrastinating again in my usual way.

She remains quiet. Thoughtful. As though some part of her already knows what is coming. But her patience doesn't last long, as I knew it wouldn't.

'It's to do with your recent absences. It has nothing to do with business, does it?' she prompts.

I shake my head, still refusing to open my eyes and meet her beautiful stare.

The final piece of the puzzle is within my grasp. I want to tell her everything and I need to share this with her. I feel that Lucrezia must reveal the remainder of her story to us both. But how to tell Lilly?

'It's regarding the past?' she asks.

'Yes.'

'And your maker?'

I gasp with relief. 'Yes.'

'I knew there was more, of course. There's been something

you've held back all along, and something I felt you were searching for as we've travelled. Although it didn't seem so urgent until we came across ...'

'Yes. In Turin. The creature that drained our strength and then followed us here. I've been afraid for you ever since. I felt I had to learn more about my origins so I could protect you.'

'All through time, man has sought to learn the answer to the question: "Where did I come from?" Why should we be any different, just because we are immortal?'

'True. But until recently I had felt no urge to explore the past at all,' I answer.

'It changed when you met me. When you met my mother too, I think.'

She understands me as always. Why had I been so afraid to share? And so I told Lilly of her ancestry. How her family tree led right back to mine. How she was a direct descendent of my daughter, Marguerite.

'You realised when you saw the letter at my parent's house? And the family tree?'

I nod.

'You've kept this secret all this time. A whole year, Gabi! Why didn't you tell me sooner?'

It had seemed so perverse to love a woman born from the blood line of my own child. And yet generations of marriages and mixing of blood made it less incestuous. Nevertheless, our relationship had been so fragile in the beginning and I had feared her flight from me night and day for the first few months.

'So, how could I tell you?'

'Even in Turin, when you told me about the loss of your children ... I thought that nothing could hurt you more than that. Surely that would have been the right moment?'

'I was still working this out myself. I spent four hundred years searching for a mate. You were the only one to survive my bite and then I learn that this could be because you have my blood in your veins.'

'Genetically we are connected. That's obvious, but why then is that relevant? Why does it matter?' she asks. 'Why do you need to know any more? We're immortal. We have nothing to fear. Looking for the reason is like learning the magician's secrets; magic is never the same again.'

For a long time I'd thought that myself. Wondered why I needed to know. In all of my existence I had never come across another immortal other than Lucrezia. The thought of my origins hadn't ever concerned me. I had been wrapped up in my obsession with finding a mate to share my life with. But now, the vampire gene in my heritage seemed so important. How did it get there? Maybe Lucrezia held the answer somewhere in her past.

'Things have changed,' I explain. 'I sought out Lucrezia for answers. And now I'm learning things that I had never guessed about her.'

'Lucrezia,' Lilly rolls the name over her tongue. 'You've never said her name to me before. Even when you told me the "graphic" details of how you were changed. I almost believed that it was a one night stand and you had never known her name.'

I look at Lilly, surprised at her thoughts. I'd never consciously omitted her name, but had obviously never thought to use it.

'Did you love her?'

I laugh. 'Lucrezia and I have had many dimensions to our limited contact, but love has never been one of them.'

'But you were lovers …'

'I was a meal to Lucrezia, nothing more.'

'Just as your victims had been to you.'

I wince at her words. Maybe Lucrezia had stalked me in much the same way I'd pursued my victims. It was hard to know and definitely didn't matter anyway. What mattered was the connection with why I had survived. And why our physical appearances were so similar.

'Lucrezia is a Borgia and I have absolutely no idea how she can be connected to my family at all. I was brought up in Florence and it seemed that my uncle Giulio, my father and my mother all grew up there too. As far as I know my grandparents were never in Rome either.'

'Lucrezia Borgia! No shit?'

'Oh. You've heard of her then?' I laugh.

'Trust you,' Lilly answers, smiling. 'You couldn't get yourself bit by any old ordinary vampire now could you? It had to be one of the most notorious women in Italian history.'

I smile. 'I think you'll get on with her like a house on fire.'

The following evening, Lilly and Lucrezia observe each other across the small round table in the café of Harvey Nichols with the scrutiny of nemeses. Their lovely expressions mimic each other. They are different and yet the same. The ancestral similarity is clearly present. I have so many questions to ask Lucrezia but it seems too early to do so. I still need to let her unfold her tale for us, and then I need to make some sense of it all.

'We're clearly all related,' Lilly points out. 'But Gabi says there's no connection to the Borgias in his family tree.'

'Yet somehow here we are,' Lucrezia says thoughtfully. 'You look so incredibly familiar to me. I can't explain why. It's almost as if ...'

'The answer may lie in your story,' I interrupt. 'You were born a hundred years before me, right?'

The old woman sitting at the table next to ours starts to choke on her milky tea and I realise that I have been speaking too loudly. Lilly and Lucrezia both giggle. I look from one to the other of them; this is way too strange, even for me.

'The surgery was very good,' Lilly puts in. 'You can't tell that you're five hundred at all.'

Lucrezia laughs louder and the people at other tables begin to look around at us. The girls smile at each other as their laughter subsides. This is going better than I expected. I feel a slight twinge as Lilly pats Lucrezia's hand.

'Gabi's told me what you've said so far. Word for word. Curse of the vampire brain, I expect. He has OCD. How about you?' Lilly takes a bite out of a caramel shortbread she's ordered. They are sickly things and have never appealed to me but Lilly loves chocolate and caramel. And now she need never worry about ruining her waistline as our weight never alters no matter how much we eat.

'Yes. I'm very OCD. I'm not sure whether it's from living alone though, or whether it is a bi-product of our condition. Your development over the next few years will be very interesting, Lilly.'

Lilly grins, and fixes Lucrezia with a stare. 'So how does the story continue? What happened to the lovely Joanna?'

Chapter 21 - Lucrezia's Story

Joanna's Blood

As I waited for her return I lay on Joanna's bed, lulled and invigorated by the moonlight as it bled through the open window. The balcony curtains shivered slightly as a night breeze wafted in. Outside in the street beyond the wall, a group of revellers passed by and began to hush each other in drunken loud whispers.

'Justice Adimari lives there. For God's sake, keep it down. Don't give any reason for his guard to come out.'

The men drifted on, sobered slightly by the realisation of the danger of the *faux pas* they almost made. I lay there wondering what I was going to do when Joanna returned. Her sheets smelt of her. The room was infused with her aura. I smelt her blood and her sensual life force as I lay like a lioness ready to pounce.

Several hours passed before she returned, tired and listless, to her room. She did not even light a candle to find her way, but merely moved across the room, discarding her clothing down to her shift. Then she slid into the bed beside me, unaware of my presence. I lay unmoving, smelling the sweet scent of red wine on her breath mingled with her youthful blood. She drifted into a deep sleep within moments.

I waited until I heard her breathing deepen and even out, and until her body was completely still. Then I rose from the bed and stood over her. I could feel my pointed fangs pricking my lower lip. They were so large and long that my gums ached. They needed blood before they would retract and I considered taking her as she slept. It would, after all, be the safest thing. But as I looked at her face, her simple prettiness charmed me and for a moment I didn't realise that she had opened her eyes and was gazing up at me.

'Beautiful fairy,' she murmured. 'Come to grant me three wishes ...'

I froze, expecting her to wake fully, to realise I was an intruder, for her screams to echo through the house. But she sighed and turned on her side as her eyes drifted closed again.

'Yes. I've come to grant you three wishes,' I whispered, kneeling beside the bed. 'But first I need a kiss.'

Joanna offered her lips like an innocent child kissing her mother. As my lips pressed against hers I felt the red lust surge through me once more. That same sensation of sexual need that drew me to take Lena's life, plunged from me into Joanna and made her swoon in my arms. Her mouth opened and I kissed her long and passionately, my tongue exploring her mouth. She tasted of red wine and brandy. She rolled onto her back and I pulled away the neckline of her chemise, exposing her slender throat and the tip of one small breast. Her hand ran through my hair and she pulled me back down to her willing mouth.

I showered kisses over her, enjoying the sensation of her pleasure which echoed back to me through every touch. It was like feeling double the passion, hers and mine. I effortlessly ripped her clothing down the middle, looked at the beauty of her pert breasts and found myself kissing and sucking them in passionate worship of her young female form. She groaned under my hands and tongue and lips. And my kisses moved lower. I wanted to explore her body in the way that I had never been permitted with another woman.

I knew the male form intimately, had been forced to pleasure it many times over. But what made a woman feel pleasure? I'd experienced moments of excitement and sensation at the hands of various lovers, but only with Caesare in the early days had I ever experienced an orgasm. I wanted to show Joanna that feeling. I wanted to pleasure her and enjoy touching her body freely in return.

My lips traced her stomach. By now my gums throbbed so much I felt physical pain. The fangs wanted to be fed, but I wanted this to last. I kissed down, remembering the loving way that Caesare had brought me like this and I kissed and licked and worshipped Joanna. She groaned and thrashed beneath me. I pulled back and looked at her. She was beautiful, neat and clean. A man would destroy that. I wanted to be her lover, wanted to be the one to take her virginity and teach her love and so I slid my finger gently inside her.

She froze a little, so I stopped and continued licking her until she opened and relaxed under me again. My finger massaged deeper; I could feel the skin there barring my way and I knew she was mine to take. Her hips rocked against my mouth as I pushed my finger further. She gasped, and bucked in pain and pleasure. I removed my finger. I smelt the blood. And I was lost.

I turned my head, burying it in her groin, where I found the vein, my fangs burying themselves deep, even as she shuddered and groaned beneath me. Her blood flooded into my mouth almost too fast for me to swallow and I gulped her down. Another orgasm shook her as I fed and her moisture gushed forward and covered my cheek as it pressed against her. And still I continued to feed, enjoying the sensation of her blood and secretions covering my face and neck, until I felt her slip into a coma beneath me.

There was no doubt in my mind that she was dead. But I lay between her legs until her body started to cool. I felt stronger again. My fangs had retracted as the blood had started to flow, no longer needed. I sat up and looked at Joanna and I knew then I really was a monster. I may as well eat babies. Nausea pulled once more at my insides.

Driven by this insane lust, I was no better than my brother. I had been led here by my need, my obsession, and I had raped and destroyed this girl. No matter how willing she had seemed, she had not understood nor consented to my intrusion. This evil power had made me into Caesare and all I wanted to do was die.

I began to moan and then to scream. The household woke and even the sound of feet running towards the room could not stop me. I threw myself on the floor and waited for the Justice and his family to enter to see what I had done to their lovely daughter, to see what sort of creature had defiled and killed her. And as they burst into the room, I continued to wail like a woman possessed.

Joanna's blood had made me insane.

Justice

News travelled fast in the countryside. The stories told of the insane woman who had murdered the Justice's beautiful daughter. I was flogged. I bled. I healed as soon as my clothing was placed over my beaten body. No one noticed, but there were rumours that I was a witch or demon. I even heard the word 'succubus' whispered through the walls of the gaol into which I was thrown. And I wondered if that was indeed what I had become.

Soon the torture began. The Justice was always present, his mouth tight as he whispered his questions to the executioner to relay to me.

'How did you get in?'

'Who helped you?'

'Why did you kill Joanna Adimari?'

'Who put you up to it?'

'Are you a witch?'

I never answered and although the torture hurt, it was bearable. They got no satisfaction from me. Even when the executioner gave me to his men, I never spoke. I let them rape me, one after another. Then they beat me, burned me with hot irons, laughed when I screamed as the fire bit viciously into my flesh. I felt I deserved to die and I wanted to test the level of pain I could endure. But their blows were little worse than the sensation of pins and needles. They couldn't hurt or injure me irreparably, no matter how much my skin blistered or how much of my blood was spilled.

'Lord,' said the executioner quietly outside my cell on one

occasion. 'We've observed some strange things about this woman, not least her ability to heal. She seems charmed.'

'She's in league with the devil,' the Justice said. 'A demon. Succubus. The only thing we can do is to burn her at the stake.'

I smiled at this. Let them do what they would. I was a monster. I deserved it.

Within a week of murdering Joanna I was taken to the town square and tied to a wooden stake mounted above a large pile of sticks and kindling. All along I knew I could escape – I doubted that even ten men could hold me – but I was unafraid. I wanted to die. I wanted to be burned and to go to hell like the evil being I was. So I allowed them to tie me up and I waited for justice to be done.

I stood before the crowd, dressed in rags, waiting for the flame to be lit. The crowd jeered and spat at me. Cries of 'witch', 'whore' and 'murderer' all floated around me, but I did not respond or look my tormentors in the eye. Instead I bowed my head and meditated. I expected to feel the pain of the fire and wanted it to purge me and purify the evil from my life. My thoughts were full of the injustice of all I had survived. But my end seemed so fitting.

I didn't notice, until he spoke, that a Catholic priest stood before me to administer the last rites. 'Do you atone for your sins?' the man asked.

'I lived in Rome, and there is no greater sinner than he who sits on the Papal seat. You hypocritical Christian, do you really think your God can save me now? Your God damned me. He gave me over to the devil to use as his concubine. I no longer believe in Him, nor worship Him. Your God made me what I am, now burn me, and be damned.'

The priest and the crowd stepped back, shocked by my words though they were delivered calmly. The crowd became more afraid and their fear vibrated through the air. I fed on it, enjoyed it. It zipped through my blood and invigorated me. My gums twitched and I felt the pricking of my fangs.

'Burn her!' someone shouted, and soon the crowd was rowdy and full of bravado.

'I killed Joanna,' I yelled above their terrified shouts. 'I fed on her blood.' I smiled a terrible smile, silencing them. 'Now burn me damn you, or I'll rise from this fragile binding and take all of your pathetic little lives, starting with your daughters.'

The torch bearer ran forward on impulse and threw his blazing torch into the pile of wood. The crowd began to cheer as the dry wood caught and the flames gathered into a rapidly spreading fire that headed straight towards me. I laughed like some sinister demon as their fear reverberated through my body feeding me every bit as potently as their blood would have.

I felt the flames lick around my ankles first, and my instinct was to tear free and run away. The fire touched the rags that covered me and quickly took flight. The clothing burned from my body, and the flames caressed my skin. It was the worst agony I had ever experienced and I howled in pain.

'Burn, demon!' the crowd roared.

The fire felt like the heat of the sun had stretched across the world and was flaying the skin from my body. I screamed again. The crowd cheered louder. I glanced down through the flames and saw my skin blacken and burn. I felt the intense agony of the exposed veins and blood beneath sizzling and cracking as the fat caught fire. Then miraculously, as fast as I burned, my skin healed. I burned again, healed again. The pain was excruciating. But always when the blood flowed, my skin healed. It was then I knew. I couldn't be burnt; I could never die. The flames were higher now, almost to my face. It burnt my breasts, my skin blacked and shrivelled as I screamed. I felt I was losing my mind from the intense and constant pain. And then my body rebuilt once more only to burn again.

It had to stop. The flame was futile. It would never destroy me. I shifted my body through the spectrum so that it became one with the fire. At the same time, a coldness seeped into my skin which stopped all aspects of the fire from eating my flesh further. To the onlooking crowd it must have seemed as though the fire had consumed me. I screamed louder for effect. But it no longer hurt at all. And then I slipped out of the charred ropes and walked down through the centre of the fire, naked, burnt and invisible. As I left the pyre my body shifted again and I became one with the dark night.

I heard the pounding of horses' hooves riding full pelt towards the pyre. I stopped and watched as a group of riders entered the square. The leader dismounted and tore off the scarf which had protected his face during the ride. It was Caesare! He stared with horror at the furiously burning fire. Already the wood was little more than glowing embers. He fell to his knees, his hands knuckled against his temples and his body shaking. I watched as he sobbed and cried at my apparent demise. Obviously he had heard the stories and realised that I must have been the cause, coming as soon as he could to try and rescue his beloved. His tears went unnoticed by the priest and the villagers as they loudly began to sing psalms as though exorcising the devil from the very air. Their zealous religion, so pathetic now to my immortal gaze, seemed like some bizarre and foreign cult. It was a fitting end to my official life.

Still cloaked in darkness I turned my back on Caesare and began to limp calmly from the village. My legs were badly burnt but each step saw them heal further and soon I was able to run. As I reached the outskirts of the town I hurried silently into the surrounding forest and away from the scene of my crime, leaving behind the ashes that would make my brother believe I was dead and would ensure my freedom away from him. As I entered the woods I glanced down at my hands and watched with fascination as the final burns healed. Joanna's sweet blood had given me more power, I was sure. It had granted me this amazing healing ability. What would my next victim do for me?

Rome

Rome greeted me silently as I instinctively lurked in shadows for fear of being recognised, despite the fact that no one could see me. The city felt alien. Even as I stepped over the threshold of the sentry point I knew I needed to leave Italy as soon as possible if I was to be certain that Caesare wouldn't hear of me again. I was afraid to be recognised for then he would learn I had survived the fire. My first thought was of finding transport quickly and then I realised I had no money to pay for passage.

Still naked, I walked along the harbour at Fumicino unseen. Invisibility had its advantages in all ways, but I was beginning to feel weaker from using it too much. I knew I would have to feed again soon. But for now I enjoyed the buzz of walking among the unique assemblage of characters that inhabited the docks. I was in the company of sailors, merchants and whores for the first time in my life. And there was a strange excitement in my heart as I realised I was seeing a world previously denied me.

I breathed in the smell of the dock. It was intoxicating. Some would say it stank. Along the pier the smell of cooked and burnt food mingled with the strong odour of rotting fish guts, which wafted from the moored fishing boats. A sailor brushed by me; his aura tasted of stale sweat and urine. I almost gagged on the stench of the place. My sense of smell was as heightened as my other senses and I had to place my hand over my mouth and nose in order to block some of the overpowering reek. Then I focused my mind to ignore it and to my pleasure the odour receded. My abilities were growing day by day.

I stood on the dock and looked around. My attention was caught by a bearded merchant in flamboyant, expensive clothing shouting instructions to a small group of young boys.

'Quicker, or I'll take the time you waste from your pay, you lazy young scoundrels,' he yelled.

The boys glanced at him. I recognised hunger in their gaunt and pale faces as they looked up at him. He'd hired them to move his wares to a cart; the boxes were heavy and they struggled to move them in their malnourished, weakened state. The merchant seemed a particularly deserving donor as my deft fingers relieved him of his substantial purse. I didn't wait to see the boys' anger when they realised he couldn't pay them, but I walked away smiling at the thought, after carefully slipping some coins into the pockets of each boy. They shivered as my fingers brushed their worn clothing but my coldness was little worse than the day offered them anyway.

Stealing was easy. Too easy. So I took more purses as I moved unseen through the harbour.

Then I began to feel tired and drained. I had to find clothing. With money that should be easy. But you had to be dressed in order to enter a store to obtain clothing. The solution eluded me for a while.

I left the docks and watched numbly as carriages and horses passed by on the road that lead into the town and further into Rome itself. I felt like a ghost looking into the world of the living but never able to enter it. It was easy to believe I didn't exist whilst invisible. As I watched the wealthy take their constitutional drives through the streets of Rome, I believed that this world was forever closed to me.

And then I saw my childhood friend Alcia. She looked much older than the last time I'd seen her, maybe five years before, and a little plumper. I followed her carriage on foot for a mile until we reached her house. Alcia had married well. But for once I did not indulge my natural curiosity. I was too afraid of being seen, or worse, succumbing to feeding from a former friend. The thought made my stomach churn. I slipped into her house unseen and in her closets and drawers found a suitable outdoor outfit, that was respectable but not ostentatious. I slipped the clothing on with some relief.

Now I could visit any tailor in the city and order clothing to furnish me with the right image I'd need for a lady travelling aboard a ship alone. I could only do that if I had money and status. A woman alone would be suspicious and so I would also need an entourage of employees. It all seemed so incredibly complicated and, as I dressed, my mind tumbled over all of the many factors that could go wrong.

Walking through the streets again, clothed and visible, I started to feel part of the world again. I wondered what would be my next move. Firstly I needed to feed my blood craving again. It was growing steadily worse with each passing day, and every time I used my invisibility I became hungrier. It affected my ability to remain rational and I began to focus on the pulsing beat at the throat of everyone I passed. It was a dangerous time. I feared losing control and turning into an insane animal. This made the need to feed far more urgent. Therefore the docks seemed the likely place to find what I needed. I reasoned that it was probably best to eat more regularly in order to avoid a lack of self control. And so I returned to the docks and hired a whore.

'I suspect this is a first for you,' I said as we went up three flights of stairs to her small and dusty room.

'A fine lady alone ... yes. But I done women plenty of times. Men like to see me with their wives and mistresses.'

'I see.' I smiled as she closed the door, and I began to peel off my black gloves. 'Take your clothes off and lie down.'

'You don't waste time,' she laughed. 'O'course stripping completely will cost you more.'

'Fine.'

The whore was younger than she seemed. Her body was firm and unscarred by childbirth. I was surprised to see this, as I assumed that she would have been pregnant at least once by now. I'd picked her for her flowing black locks and laughing brown eyes. She seemed sweet natured, though I was certain she was experienced. I'd thought her pretty, but there was a hardness around her eyes that made her seem harsh in certain light.

She stripped and lay on the bed as I watched and her nakedness excited me. But now I recognised why; the sensation was less about her body, and more about the fine blue veins that threaded her olive skin, just under the surface. Her stomach muscles were taut and firm, her breasts pert. I watched the blood pump under her fine skin, followed its pathway all the way to her heart. My stomach growled.

I walked towards her with the gait of a predator.

'What's your name?' I asked seconds before my fangs extended from my gums and into her neck.

I fed on her blood until her eyes dulled and she sank into death with ecstatic orgasmic cries strangling her last breath. And I so wanted more. My nails were like talons and I ripped open her chest at the last moment. She didn't feel it; she was already comatose. But I wanted to suck the last beat from her heart, and I snapped the arteries as I pulled it free.

I pressed my greedy mouth against the still spasming muscle and swallowed her last drops. I licked my fingers clean of her blood. Then I lay back on her bed like a decadent whore myself, my body jerking and rolling with the ecstacy of her vital blood rushing through me, its vibrancy shivered through every nerve ending until late into the night.

Chapter 24 - Lucrezia's Story

Whore

I was determined to enjoy Rome's underbelly, though I instinctively lurked in the shadows. The lowlife, the evil, rank world of the poor, held a bizarre fascination for me. If you visited the dock alone as a woman, you were liable to be raped. If you hired a whore, she may rob you of your purse as you slept. If you drank in the taverns then sailors would offer you money for a good time. This was the world of the dock. Its rules were uncomplicated and the simple honesty of the lowest dregs of humanity was refreshing.

The world of wealth, the world I'd known as the daughter of a Pope, had been full of sin, evil and debauchery. It was false. No one was really your friend; declarations of love would be denied days later once lovers had satisfied their lust. No one could be trusted. A pregnancy would be hushed up and the girl sent away to be married off as a virgin at the first opportunity. This had been my life. This was why I took over the life of the whore on the docks, why I disposed of her body and began to wear her clothes and live in her room. This is how I became known as 'Juliet the whore', who gave her customers the best time and never stole from them. Of course I did steal something from them, although their memory of it was always very vague. They remembered the ecstasy of my touch. And I didn't have to kill if I took only a little blood each night. It was far less conspicuous than murder, even in this lawless society.

The sailors always wanted more of a good thing, and they came back for it. I built up a regular clientele and actually began to enjoy the seedy and violent life of the underworld I had once been afraid of. Even the strange requests and sexual perversities of my clients interested me. I took part in them as though they were some form of experiment.

The most surprising thing was how the docklands accepted me wholeheartedly: men more readily than the other whores at first.

'You're new around here, and there are rules you have to play by,' a sassy whore of about forty told me.

'Rules?'

'Yeah. And this here is my patch.'

'I see.'

It was a quiet night. There hadn't been a new ship for several days, which meant trade was slow. The whores were squabbling over every potential customer. It had been noted that I had more than average success, even though the younger girls were usually the busiest.

'So what's your name then?' asked the whore, her hand on her hip. I noticed the other whores carefully watching our exchange.

'I'm Juliet,' I answered automatically. 'Who are you?'

'I'm Margo. And I run this area. Like I said, there's a way things are done around here.'

I looked around at the others. I read curiosity, but not fear, from their thoughts. Margo was respected. The code among the whores was that they looked after each other.

'Well, Margo. I'm new in town and I could do with some good advice,' I said. 'It's a slow night, so why don't we go get some drinks in the tavern. I'm paying if you've a mind for the company and are willing to explain things to me.'

Margo's arm dropped from her hip and her stance became benign. In the end friendship and generosity were all that anyone needed. I became accepted as one of them and I was always ready to pay for cheap wine for my new friends. Because whores disappeared daily, the old Juliet was soon forgotten and no one, not even the landlord, asked where she was.

At first I found it sad that no one seemed to care, but it was also freeing. This was a world that required no explanation. A lovely, welcoming world. To be different was to be one of them. I stayed there for two years exploring and tasting the underworld of Rome. It was never tiresome. I lost my ladylike manners as I mimicked my peers.

'Juliet!' yelled Margo from the doorway of *The Shuttered Door*, one of the more popular taverns. 'Watch out for the Cap'n o' the *Celestine*, he likes to rough his girls up and I heard he was looking for you earlier. He's been through all of us at some time or other. He messed up Justina so bad she hasn't worked for a month.'

Anger flared in my chest. I recalled the brutality of my brother. The thought of little Justina being abused by some brute made my stomach churn. Although I hadn't seen her around, it was vexing to realise she had been injured and couldn't work.

'Don't worry, lovey,' I replied. 'I know just how to handle his sort.'

The Captain found me in the tavern. Once we were alone he received a beating he'd never forget and would never admit was delivered by a woman. I suspect he told his crew he was set upon by thugs. Five of them at least. I left him alive, barely.

'Stay away from the whores of Fumicino,' I hissed in his ear. 'And stay your fists in future unless you want me to finish this. Believe me, I'll know if you hurt another woman.'

He'd stared in swollen-eyed horror at my lengthened fangs. His mind screamed 'demon' but he was too afraid to speak. He emptied his bowels into his breeches. Just for show, I laughed manically to ensure his view of an avenging monster was forever burnt into what passed for his brain. I also made sure that Justina received a financial boost from a mysterious benefactor. I knew she had five children and struggled to feed them while trying to make the best living she could. With money to feed and clothe herself, she soon recovered and was back in the docks working alongside Margo and the others again.

It was easy to believe I was one of them, that I finally belonged somewhere. Now I was both visible and invisible; hidden in the most conspicuous world. This was a place that the wealthy knew existed, the corrupt used and enjoyed, and the pious chose to ignore.

The most difficult times were when wealthy friends I'd known in my old world came to the dock looking for a cheap thrill. I'd seen a few familiar counts, a duke and even a prince and, as Juliet, had serviced them all. I'd been careful to keep my fangs in check on these occasions. Strangely, they never recognised me. I think it was in part my youthful transformation. I also suspected that in some part of their brains, they couldn't acknowledge recognition of a fellow aristocrat fallen low.

Being a whore thrilled me. I did not see it as shameful. Besides, it was my choice. I didn't have to live this life for the money but because I chose to, and therefore I picked my clients carefully. I only fucked and bled those I found desirable. This was how I came to move into the next stage of my life.

A young count, who I didn't know, arrived at the docks with his new wife, a beautiful and fragile woman of eighteen. I watched them enter the tavern with the same trepidation as others. Once I laid eyes on his wife, I knew I had to have her.

The count had brought her there for instruction. It was a common occurrence: a young sophisticated and inexperienced man with an inexperienced wife.

'I'm Juliet,' I said, looking deep into his eyes.

His cock hardened in his trousers as I stroked his arm, sending lust into his body.

'You are exactly what we need,' he answered.

I took them to my rooms. The woman was quiet. I could smell her nervous perspiration. He'd obviously told her his expectations and though she was unwilling, the guilt at her inadequacy would make her comply. I knew this sort of man. All he wanted was to lie back and be serviced. He would give no thought to his wife's pleasure at all.

'Ariadne,' he said, as he began to strip. 'Take off my boots.'

She obeyed.

'I want you to watch how the whore does things to me, and this is what I expect of you. Do you understand?' There was a threat in his tone. I glanced at the girl. She nodded, very afraid. Interesting. I wondered if he had hurt her, or had at least threatened to.

He removed his clothing, insisting she help whenever he wanted it. Made her unfasten his breeches, slipping them down his legs until she was eye level with his groin. He looked at me then and gestured.

'Teach her to suck it,' he commanded.

I smiled. I really didn't like his attitude and this lovely little girl deserved so much better.

'I will. But, good sir, I have some other tricks that may interest you more.'

'I'm an experienced man,' he lied.

'I don't doubt it. But the only way to learn how to give pleasure is to receive it.'

He weighed me up. 'What do you mean?'

I gestured towards Ariadne.

'I can show your wife how to enjoy sex, and then she will enjoy servicing you and will be better at satisfying your needs. Lovemaking is not just about fulfilling a lust, it's about sensual touch, kissing, stroking. Adoring your lover's body.'

While I spoke I stroked his arm. Then let my hand wander over his bare chest, and down his belly, stroking small seductive circles that almost touched his rapidly hardening cock.

'Oh my God,' he gasped.

I saw the light of lust flame in his black pupils. Any moment now, he would try to take me. I continued to flush my power through his skin, leaving a burning trail of sex everywhere I touched. I stopped attending to him and turned to Ariadne. The air crackled with sexual energy now. She shivered with fear and slight anticipation as my hand closed over hers. I pulled her to me.

'This is how you must kiss your wife,' I told him. I took her in my arms, my mouth consumed her and my tongue filled her. To my pleasure, Ariadne was a fast learner. She kissed me back eagerly, her body trembling with excitement. I kissed her pink lips until they flushed red. All the time, I stroked her back lightly.

'This is how you undress your wife.'

I stripped her slowly. Each piece of her expensive satin clothing was peeled away, followed by kisses and strokes. Unlacing her bodice, I kissed her breasts as they tumbled out into my eager and gentle fingers. I sucked on her nipples until she threw her head back. Her knees buckled. I held her up, steadied her and resumed my attention, while beside us her husband sank down on the edge of the bed in fascination.

I had her naked now and I passed her to him. He mimicked my moves, kissing and sucking her nipples gently. Her body rocked against him with renewed pleasure. She obviously loved him. He was beautiful, as was she. I could see that his experience until now had all been about his satisfaction. It had never occurred to him that making a woman moan with excitement was equally gratifying.

He wanted to take her, but I wouldn't let him; it was too soon. I showed him how to kiss down her body. I spread her on the bed and kneeled between her open legs. Here I licked and sucked her until she cried out, thrashing beneath me.

'Ariadne,' he moaned, pushing me aside. He copied me again until her fevered cries culminated in screams of orgasm. She shuddered beneath him. Only then did I let him enter her.

He lay above her, looking into her eyes. She was swooning with the shock of her sexual release. He fumbled around her eagerly until his cock found the entrance. He thrust hard into her. She arched her back with pain and some residue of pleasure but it was too much.

'Slow down,' I said. 'Draw back slowly, and then plunge.'

He did as I suggested. The joy and passion on Ariadne's face as he took her spurred him on to gradually increase his movements. The harder and faster he became the more her screams of excitement increased. She dug her nails in him, writhing beneath him like the whore he wanted. Yet, the pleasure was mutual.

'Larenzo,' she sobbed against him. 'Oh please, don't stop.'

As he spent himself, she exploded once more. Fully satisfied, fully loved, they lay wrapped in each other's arms stroking and touching. It was the most beautiful sight I had ever seen.

They eventually left after paying me handsomely. I had discovered a new calling.

Chapter 25 - Present

Sex Therapist

'News spread far and wide after that,' Lucrezia smiles, sipping her coffee.

'So, basically, you became a sex therapist? In the sixteenth century?' Lilly asks, her eyes wide and round with admiration.

Lucrezia laughs. 'Yes, I guess so. I ended up doing more of that than whoring afterwards. It seemed to me that men really needed to learn to understand a woman's needs.'

'Oh my fucking God! You were a feminist before your time,' Lilly giggles. 'I like you so much already.'

I feel a little twinge as the girls smile at each other. A small amount of jealousy will do me good, I suppose. I can't help thinking that Lilly is mine, and I don't really care to share her. Luci looks at me as though she hears my thoughts. I slam my shields down.

'I like you too,' she responds to Lilly. 'In fact it is very satisfying being around my own kind. I've buried myself among humans for a long time.'

'Haven't we all.'

Luci and Lilly look at me. Lilly's eyes are round with wonder as she turns her gaze back to Lucrezia.

'I think you have suffered a great deal,' Lilly observes. 'Both of you. But you've come out of it well. Eternity is a frightening prospect. You've both faced it alone and survived as best you can. I feel so lucky right now.'

'You are lucky,' Luci smiles. 'Gabi loves you so very much. It's something I denied myself all these years. Yes, I've coped. I've had very little social life though, other than my occasional dip into the world of humanity. It's easy to become isolated when you don't have anyone you can be truly honest with.'

'Haven't you loved at all?' I ask.

'Oh yes. In a fashion ...'

Chapter 26 - Lucrezia's Story

Gypsy

My little world in Rome ticked by without much incident. I thought perhaps that I could stay there forever unnoticed. I had a new brand of clientele. And they paid well to learn the art of love. I recalled a book in my father's study, *The Kama Sutra*. With my increasing wealth I managed to procure a copy from a travelling merchant.

By then I had a small house, and I decorated it with eastern furniture. Chaise lounges of red satin, billowing reams of silk draped around the room. Cushions, beautifully beaded in lovely bright colours, scattered the floor of my main 'treatment' room. I had trays of exotic middle-eastern foods, such as Turkish pastes flavoured with fruit oils, on platters. Incense burned on gold plates. I bought all of these things from the merchant Captains at the docks. It was a sort of therapy for me, and I did see myself as a doctor, I suppose, helping her patients. Even though some of those patients were sexually dysfunctional couples.

Mostly I helped young and inexperienced couples who recommended to their friends that they should visit me, promising them ultimate happiness with their new spouse. My skills were advertised and promoted by word of mouth. It was always the men that instigated it, often with the misguided view that they would come away with their wife learning skills that would pleasure them. They each wanted to possess the ultimate virgin-whore. Yes, the wives learned plenty about the art of lovemaking, but never on the first few visits. The men learned instead. I applied the philosophies of the Indian book to teach them love and to encourage respect for their wives.

My customers were always happy, especially the women. I felt that although my life was much changed, somehow fate had brought me here to help them; to guide these women so that they would not experience the unhappiness that I had suffered. Perhaps it was stupid and misguided, maybe even arrogant of me to think that the universe had some design to make me the saviour of my gender. Yet it was a thought that floated frequently through my mind.

I devised a new background for myself; naturally my clients were curious. I was Juliet, daughter of a sea captain who had travelled the world. I told them I had been born in India. They believed I had been raised in an exotic world that saw love and passion as the norm. Superstitiously they believed that I held some mystical knowledge that would bring them ultimate happiness. It was certainly true that I was charismatic and I used my vampiric hypnosis to relax them.

I stopped feeding from my clients because now that I was more legitimate it would be an unnecessary risk. Instead I used passing sailors to sate my hunger. I did try to disguise myself. I'd obtained clothing that matched those worn by the women in the *Kama Sutra* book. I'd been told that these garments were called 'saris'. They consisted of a long flowing skirt and cropped top, which was then covered with vibrantly coloured silks. I wrapped the silk around my midriff and wore it pinned like a veil to my head, while my hair fell free over my shoulders. In a way I worried about my new image, though I tried to pretend it made me appear anything other than Lucrezia. An anonymous whore could be forgotten. 'Indian Juliet' however, had become distinctive and it seemed for a time that I was invulnerable because my new persona was so accepted.

Then, everything changed completely.

I was taking my normal stroll along the waterfront, a habit I'd retained. The morning was bright but cool. I'd grown used to the sounds and smells there. I secretly loved seeing the whores I'd befriended. The atmosphere was always the same. It was only the faces that changed. I hadn't forgotten my friends; I regularly sent money and gifts to Margo and Justina but they never knew they came from me. I preferred it that way. It was easier that they thought I'd moved on and forgotten them.

Along the pier I paused and looked out to sea. A few miles offshore a huge cargo ship was approaching and I hoped it was the one I was waiting for. If so, it would contain a new consignment of silks to make my Indian outfits from and boxes of the Turkish sweets that my clients enjoyed. I stood, breathing in the sea air. The smells of the dock were both vile and endearing all at once. There was an underlying stench of rotting fish guts coming from the fish stalls, where the innards were scraped out, discarded underfoot and left to rot. Every few days the floor was swilled by sea-water, the remains swept into the sea.

I was hypnotised by the gentle crash of the waves against the hull of the ship as it drew painfully slowly towards the dock. For a moment I became unaware of any movement around me.

Then I saw the gypsy. She had luscious flowing long black curls. Her multicoloured skirt and bodice were tightly stretched over a firm and sensuously curved body. She was beautiful. Her dark eyes fell in my direction, but I knew she couldn't see me; I was still cloaked. She was leaning against the side of a small boat that was upended on the dock, watching the world pass by in much the same way as I was.

What surprised me was that no one seemed to notice her. It was as if she too was invisible. A beautiful woman standing on the dock would rarely remain unaccosted for long, even if it was merely the flirty comments of passing sailors. Yet she stood unobserved as people passed by. I was only a few yards away but I edged closer.

I studied her emerald coloured sash and her scarf, which had tiny coins sewn on to it. The sash was tied around her hips and over a flared purple skirt. The scarf was tied around her raven hair.

She stared in my direction, her eyes narrowing. I turned and looked behind to see what she was looking at.

'I'm looking at you,' she said.

I breathed in sharply.

'You think you can hide from the hidden?'

'What do you mean?' I asked, stepping forward. I must have let my cloaking slip somehow.

'No, you are still hidden to others, but not to me.'

I scrutinised her beautiful, sharp features. Her eyes were intensely green, not black as I had first thought, and her cheekbones and nose were classically chiselled. She was exotic and stunning to look at.

'You can read my mind?' I asked.

She shrugged.

'I have my skills. I know what you are, but you needn't be afraid. I'm no threat to you.'

I felt speechless for the first time in years. I could only stare at her as she gazed back at me, her expression curious but warm.

'I'm Miranda,' she said, smiling. 'Would you like me to read your palm?'

I let her lead me away from the docks and out along the road. There stood a barrel-shaped coach with a sturdy grey horse harnessed to it. Miranda patted the horse.

'This is Bellina,' she told me. 'She's a faithful companion, a strong and sturdy animal. She has been with me for many years and adventures.' I followed Miranda around to the back of the carriage where a set of steps lead up to a doorway. 'This is my home.'

Of course I'd heard of the Romany Gypsies and their nomadic lives. As an aristocrat I had been among the privileged few that could afford fortune-tellers, though I had never used one. Perhaps my religious upbringing had always made me wary of the supernatural. Now I knew I had nothing to fear. Miranda could not hurt me. I was fascinated to understand how she knew who and what I was. I followed her into her caravan.

Inside appeared bigger than the outside, as if enchanted. It was tidy and compact. At the far end was a bunk covered in furs, silks and cushions. It looked like the most comfortable bed, but also would serve as a couch. Miranda lifted up a table that had been laid flat to the side of wall. As it unfolded, a hinged leg extended to give it support, and with a little adjustment she secured it. It took up half of the space in the caravan. She indicated a stool. I sat numbly opposite her, wondering what she would find when she looked at my palm.

Miranda held out her hand to me and I gave her mine after a moment's hesitation. She looked into my face as she touched my skin for the first time, her eyes widening slightly. I wondered what she observed about my skin that caused that reaction. As though reading my mind again, she shrugged.

'You feel smooth and cool. Unique.'

Her hand felt strange to me also, though I couldn't understand why. Even so, I didn't question her further. I was intent on watching her expression as her gaze fell to studying my outstretched hand.

'Curious,' she said. 'I can't read you at all. There are no lines, not as there should be. I will need to consult my cards.'

She turned away and from behind her she retrieved a beautiful, polished oak box, and opening it quickly withdrew a pack of cards, wrapped up in a blue velvet cloth. She opened the fabric and handed the cards to me.

'Cut them. Shuffle if you know how.'

'Show me how and I will.'

She quickly shuffled the cards, splitting them with skilled and effortless practice, then placed them in my hand. I mimicked her perfectly. She smiled. Once cut, I placed the cards before her as she indicated.

She picked them up and, taking cards from the top, began to lay them in a complex pattern before me. Ten in all.

'This card is you,' she said, and turned the indicated card over.

I saw that these were no ordinary playing cards, but were completely distinctive. This card pictured a hooded figure holding a scythe.

'Death,' she explained. 'As I thought. But don't be afraid, it doesn't predict death; quite the opposite. In your case, it means rebirth.'

She flipped over the next card. I looked at it long and hard. It showed a crumbling tower. I couldn't derive any meaning at all from it.

'This represents your current life. It tells me that you are living in a falsely secure world. But soon it must end.'

Several more cards were turned, and all pointed towards me urgently needing to leave.

'But why?'

Miranda shrugged, then turned the final card. It showed a man, clothed flamboyantly and holding a wand. Around him stars exploded.

'This is the magician. Usually it represents someone who is persuasive. It can mean you are going to be coerced, maybe conned out of money or jewellery. In its current position it is far more serious. This man is linked to your past. He is evil, corrupt and will stop at nothing to possess you again. Lucrezia, you need to leave Rome. Your brother is coming.'

The Magician

I sat upright in my bed; the intensity of the dream shook me. Miranda was so vivid in my mind that I really believed I had met her and she had read my fortune. Instinctively I knew that the cards were called Tarot and although I was sure I had never seen them before, I was certain that at some time I must have heard the conversation or read the thoughts of someone who had. Blood gave me many images when I took it. I was sure that the mind of some sailor I'd fed from recently had provided me with the image and name of the gypsy, maybe even the glimpse of her cards. But even as I reasoned this out, my stomach churned at the echo of her warning. As I lay shivering in my bed, I believed for a brief moment that Caesare was coming. Somehow he'd learnt I was alive.

It was early morning. I decided to go for a walk to clear my head. I found myself at the docks. Walking the path of my dream was a form of exorcism. I saw the upturned boat, but no gypsy woman leaning on it and I smiled at my own silliness. I, an immortal, had been burnt at the stake and survived. How on earth could a dream cause me so much anxiety? For that matter, how could Caesare still hold any fear for me? He couldn't possibly know of my existence.

The dock was busy. A new ship had recently arrived. The dock labourers were unloading crates onto a large carriage while several dock urchins were running around their legs offering help for a few coins. I glanced at the boxes as I walked past. The workers didn't acknowledge me any more than they did the urchins; I was cloaked from their mortal vision. But as I passed by, one of the boxes drew my attention. Pasted on the side was a poster. It looked like the tarot card of the magician in my dream: A man with a wand surrounded by exploding stars.

My heart thumped. I was deluding myself. The only person in the world I needed to fear was Caesare. He would most certainly have the same strength and power as I did. Was this a premonition that he was coming to Rome and that if I stayed he would find me?

I hurried away from the dock back towards my house. As I turned the final corner I saw a carriage I didn't recognise pulling up outside my home. Instinct made me fall back against the wall and I cloaked myself quickly.

I watched and waited for the occupants to alight. A man stepped down; grey haired and official, leaving the door of the carriage open behind him. He rang the doorbell and my servant, old Federico, answered the door. My keen hearing picked up the exchange.

'My client would like a discreet appointment with *Senora* Juliet,' the man said.

'Unfortunately the *Senora* is not home,' Federico explained. 'But if you would care to leave a card, the *Senora* will most certainly send word of when she is available.'

Another man stepped from the carriage, tall, slender, feline.

My world stopped. I would have recognised him anywhere. He was my greatest fear realised.

'I will wait for her return,' Caesare said, his voice strong and clear and he walked into my house before Federico could make any objection.

'Oh no.' I backed away as the door closed behind him and the other man returned to the carriage.

Caesare had found me. He knew I was alive. But how?

I turned and hurried back down the street towards the dock and as far away from my house as I could get. All the time praying that Caesare could not sense me and would not pursue right away. My immediate plan was to stow away on a ship. It would be easy to remain invisible and, to maintain my strength, feed on the sailors as they slept. As I rounded the corner I saw the gypsy caravan from my dream driving full pelt towards me.

'Get inside!' Miranda yelled as she pulled up before me. 'He felt your presence and he's on his way.'

There was no time to ask any questions. I hurled myself inside the caravan, barely registering that it was identical in every detail to my dream. It could so easily have been a trap set up by my brother, but although I knew it was insane, I trusted Miranda. I heard her click her tongue, flick the reins, and the horse broke into a rapid gallop heading out of Rome and away from Caesare once more.

The caravan interior felt strange. There was something silent and timeless about it. As I closed the door behind me the air rippled with magic. I was aware of Miranda driving and of the rocking movement of the carriage, but these seemed like distant events. At the speed with which she drove I should have been tossed around, yet I could walk without difficulty. I tried to sense the world outside, but finding I could not, I sat down on the bunk and waited for answers.

The bunk was as comfortable as it looked. I lay and dozed fitfully for an hour or so until I felt the caravan slow and come to a halt. After a moment, the door opened and Miranda entered. She smiled at me wickedly.

'I'll light a fire and we'll rest here tonight,' she said.

'But it's only morning. Shouldn't we keep driving?' As I spoke I looked beyond her and saw the twilight framed by the doorway. 'You're a witch!' I gasped.

'Of course I am,' she laughed. Then she turned and walked outside.

It took me a moment to come to terms with what seemed to be the sudden change of time of day. The atmosphere in the caravan had altered. The hollow noiseless feeling was gone with the opening of the door. Eventually I stood and stepped down from the cabin and out into a barren clearing off what appeared to be a main highway.

'Where are we?' I asked as I watched her positioning sticks and kindling for a fire.

'A long way from Rome.'

I stared around me. The terrain seemed distinctly different. A few miles away I saw a vineyard of red grapes. The land on which it stood stretched beyond my view but I suspected we were many miles away from Rome, more distance than we could possibly have travelled in the space of one day.

'You're safe. Your brother cannot find you while you are with me.'

I scrutinised Miranda. She was an enigma I had no way of understanding quickly.

'I didn't dream meeting you, did I?'

Miranda laughed easily again. 'The caravan protects me. A by-product of having visited it is that memories of me become confused and vague. Most people forget completely; but then, you are not most people are you?'

'You know what I am?'

Miranda nodded.

'And yet you saved me. Why?'

'My palm path predicted it,' she answered, glancing down at her own hand. 'I have no choice but to follow my destiny if I am to return to my past.'

'What do you mean?'

Her words confused me. She merely shrugged in response.

'Bring out the stools,' she ordered once the fire was burning vibrantly.

Obeying, I fetched them from the caravan, placing them beside the fire as she unhooked a bag that hung from the side of the door. It contained pans and she began to prepare food while singing hypnotically. She was the most fascinating creature I had ever met.

'I can teach you many things,' she told me as she handed me

a bowl of stew. 'Most importantly right now is how to hide from him. He knows you are alive.'

'How did he find me?'

Miranda gazed into the flames of the fire for a long time watching . She watched them dance. Curious, I looked too. I wanted to see what she saw.

'It was a chance remark from a Count he knows. The man told him of the miracle you had worked on his relationship with his new wife.'

'I suppose rumour would reach him; referral was how I obtained my clients after all. I should have remained anonymous.'

'No. You are a healer by nature. It was instinct for you to use what knowledge you had in order to help others.'

I looked at Miranda, expecting sarcasm in her eyes. Her expression was serious and sincere.

'I'm a blood sucking monster. I've killed people. Aren't you afraid?' I asked finally.

'No. You will not kill me.'

I didn't ask her how she knew, yet I was certain at that moment that she was right. She was the last person in the world I would ever want to destroy.

Chapter 28 - Lucrezia's Story

Miranda

Miranda was a Romany witch. She knew all the secrets of herbs. Her knowledge of plants and their healing properties was endless, and in me she had an excellent pupil. My vampiric mind was able to retain information, and with my natural logic I questioned her incessantly about her knowledge of immortality. Regardless of that we travelled for months before I asked her about the pentagram symbol.

'Its evil, isn't it?'

Miranda laughed. 'Of course not. It's a powerful image but it can be used for good or evil. It depends on the way it's used. The pentagram is a complimentary empowerment symbol. It can be used just as effectively to charge up a healing potion as it can be used to enforce a curse.'

I considered her words carefully. My brother had used the symbol to empower his curse. He had turned me into a monster, all for his own sick pleasure.

'Can it be used to make me human again?'

Miranda was sewing beads onto a piece of silk she'd traded for in a small town we'd passed through. She stopped and looked at me.

'Why would you want that?'

I shrugged. I wasn't sure I did want mortality again. But it seemed I needed to know and understand all the possibilities. I was dressed as she was now and she had taught me to dance, a powerful erotic swaying of the hips and belly. The coins on our hip sashes jingled, creating music from our movements.

'Mortals have sought the elixir of life for all time,' she explained.

'Don't see this as a curse. It is a gift. You will live far into the future and see the world evolve into a magical time. That magic will be science. Real magic will be lost as we know it. The world will become one of unbelievers. But you! You are the living essence of magic and you'll survive the ravages of time forever.'

'You make it sound romantic! But it's terrifying.'

Miranda nodded. 'Yes, but you'll survive, Luci. You will find a place for your empathy. Now draw the symbol in the dirt.'

I did as she asked, and my magic instruction took a new turn.

'Not that way,' she said, taking a thin stick from the pile beside the fire. 'Like this.'

She drew the symbol starting with the top point, then indicated that I should copy her.

'The pentagram feels like it belongs on my tongue, under my hands,' I said.

'It was used during your making; it is a symbol of power for you. Here is another, stronger image.

Miranda drew a motif in the dirt. It was shaped like an eye and held in its centre a three-branched shape.

'In the centre is a triskele,' she told me. 'It means re-birth and renewal. The three circles around it represent the number of all magic. Three is the number of fertility: the most powerful magic of all.'

'I did have many children,' I explained.

'Yes, and they are important. Your first to your last, and your vampiric child is going to be the most crucial to your very existence.'

I laughed. 'I cannot become pregnant now.'

'Not in the true sense, but nevertheless you will procreate.'

She finished sewing the scarf and passed it to me. I swirled it around my hair, dismissing her words immediately. I had to hide my blonde locks; we feared the rumour of a fair-haired gypsy reaching my brother's spies who roamed the country. Miranda told me that Caesare did indeed have the power to create revenant servants to do his bidding. They were his eyes and ears. He was far more powerful than I could possibly imagine.

'Did Caesare sell his soul to the devil?' I asked.

'In a way. But things are never that simple. The devil is a creation of the Christian faith and he emulates our Pagan horned God in appearance. This is how the priests justify that my beliefs are evil. My God is the consort of a beautiful Goddess, and she, not the male God, created all of nature. Magic is all around us, Luci. Can't you feel it ripping through your hair in the wind? Can't you smell it in the sting of the rain? Surely you can feel it's power in the intensity of the sun?

A breeze picked up as she spoke, whipping at my scarf, and a straggling blonde curl flicked free until the wind suddenly dropped. Miranda laughed as I tucked it back in. She spoke in riddles and rarely answered my questions directly. When Miranda was in the mood, she told me all about her world and her beliefs. The stories of the Goddess and her consort were the most beautiful ones I'd ever heard. It made more sense to believe her version of creation. We would often debate the content of the bible against her knowledge and faith.

'I'm not saying that your faith is entirely false,' she said during one conversation. 'Some of it was born from my own. Often the rituals you observe have come from the ceremonies the Pagans derived centuries before. The problem with Christianity is that men, and not women, are in charge.'

I laughed but Miranda looked at me sternly. She meant what she said and so I fell quiet and listened to her talk.

'Men, particularly ones who profess religion, are the most corrupt.'

I couldn't argue. I'd seen it in my own household. I stroked Miranda's arm as she spoke and cuddled up beside her as though we were lovers. I was besotted with her. But we were never sexually intimate. Although she kissed and petted me like a mother or sister, our relationship never went in an erotic direction. It never occurred to me until later to wonder why. I loved her more than I'd ever loved anyone. My life soon began to revolve around her.

Chapter 29 - Lucrezia's Story

Becoming More

'You're a vampire,' Miranda told me as we camped on the outskirts of a French town. 'But you are not a monster. Monsters have no emotions. They kill and think nothing of it. But you have stopped killing; you feed to live.'

'I've told myself this over and over, but none of it makes sense. What are we and why do we exist? How did this all happen?'

Miranda shook her head, a smile playing across her mouth. 'Your questions are no different than those of humanity, Luci. As for the answers to them: that will take a long journey of discovery. Many hundreds of years will pass first.'

'Will I live on?' I asked. 'And never age?'

She nodded. The fire was glowing on her dark hair, it seemed to absorb the light, and her eyes held a faint golden glint. Sometimes she looked familiar. I'd spent hours scrutinising her face trying to determine her ancestry. She knew so much and, for a mortal, she was afraid of nothing. She never grew sick or seemed to age. I was intensely curious about her, but she only ever told me what she wanted me to know. Her mind was impenetrable, though she had no trouble at all reading mine.

We were together for seven full years. During that time I fed carefully from chosen victims in the various towns that we visited. As we travelled, Miranda taught me all she knew about magic.

'You know almost everything that I know,' she said. Her eyes held the mystery of centuries. I suspected that she would always be one step ahead of me no matter how much I learned.

'Vampire,' I said. 'But what does that mean?'

Miranda laughed.

'You look for philosophy where there is none. Sometimes things just are. You must know that Caesare was not the first.'

I did know that. I was certain that he must have been turned. Even so, I'd thought it through over and over. I recalled, and now understood, the words of magic he'd used during the ceremony. I often wondered who his maker was.

'None of that matters,' Miranda sighed. 'He might as well have wasted his breath. You had to change. It was in your blood.'

'How so?'

'Does the leech ask why he lives? Does the deer cry as the hunter takes him down, wondering why he must die?'

'I don't know what you are saying; you talk in riddles.'

'There are some things that happen that cannot be explained,' said Miranda, remaining enigmatic. 'At least not until the time is right. You are not ready for this knowledge. But know this: Vampires are like the burning sun. Without somewhere to shine, their glow is pointless. You are a fire that will never die, even when the earth crumbles to dust.'

It was strange how I reverted so easily to pupil from teacher. Miranda's words gave me new power. Her magic instruction imparted to me the knowledge to protect myself from humans and supernatural beings alike.

'If I'm a healer,' I asked, hanging out our washing on hooks that protruded from the caravan, 'then teach me healing magic.'

'All magic is healing, Luci, even fire. You just need to focus it to your needs.'

Miranda taught me nine basic magical potions.

'Three times three is the most powerful number, Luci.'

To begin with she raised the cloth that covered the bunk we slept on and withdrew a large black pot.

'Basic tools of magic,' she told me. 'A potion and words of power.'

We created a healing lotion. Miranda explained how the

ointment could be used just as easily to hurt as to heal.

'The intention is what counts.'

The potions took the form of ointments, lotions, medicines and tonics. With those nine, thousands of spells could be created. There were nine words of power too, which could be used in various ways. It seemed that all that was needed was the thought or wish behind the spell to make it work.

'Words of power are specific to the individual,' she explained. 'My own words would probably do nothing for you at all. The triskele I showed you is a potent word and symbol for your kind, Luci. Use it wisely, one day it may save your life.'

'And the pentagram?'

'Yes. All witches use the pentagram, it is the one symbol we have in common.'

Miranda stirred the pot. She was making a protection spell. I'd learnt that she renewed the wards on the caravan on the first day of every new moon.

'The moon gives us power. And for a vampire ...' She looked up into my eyes as she spoke and I stopped fidgeting with my coin belt and gazed back at her. 'The moon gives you a source of nourishment if you know how to tap into it.'

I waited as she returned to her stirring. It would have been like her to stop there and not explain further. When she was in that mood nothing in the world could induce her to speak. This time she looked up again, as though remembering to finish her explanation.

'Have you ever danced naked in it, Luci?'

I laughed. 'Like a real witch?'

Miranda smiled. 'Yes like a "real" witch! And like a true vampire. You see, there are many ways to feed.'

With that she grew silent again.

'In my old life,' I said, 'there were many forms of vampire. And by that I mean parasites that preyed on those weaker than themselves. My brother was a monster long before he grew fangs.'

'He couldn't help himself,' Miranda replied. 'Destiny had a hand in all of it. Everything that has happened to you since the day you were born has led to this moment. Caesare will learn his own lessons, and there will be a price to pay for his crimes.'

I believed her words. I felt the air ripple with her curse. I knew that somehow, in some distant time, Caesare would wear the burden of his felony.

'What we sow, we reap?' I asked.

Miranda nodded. 'In a fashion. But the universe has a design for it all.'

'Miranda... that day, the day you came for me. How did you know? Nothing you have shown me so far has even touched on the level of knowledge that you had that day. How did you know so much about the past, present and future?'

'My dear Luci. That is the destiny I had to fulfil, just as your tuition was my ultimate task. And now you are almost ready to go back into the world. You are almost ready to face your demons and live the life you were destined to.'

I felt ready – almost. I knew I could hide my presence from my brother now. Even if we stood in the same room I could be masked from him. The spell of protection Miranda had taught me seemed like my most valuable weapon. I felt safe in the knowledge that he could never find me.

'We'll face the world together.' I smiled. 'And what a powerful force we'll make.'

I hugged Miranda as though my life depended on it. Maybe I suspected, even then, that she would not remain with me forever. She was mortal, after all. Age and death would come to her one day, despite the magic I assumed she must use to keep her youthful looks.

Despite my vague intuition, nothing could prepare me for the day I woke to find that she had gone. The caravan, the horse and Miranda were lost from my life as suddenly as they had arrived. I never saw my friend and mentor again.

Medici

I was shocked and hurt by Miranda's desertion. Her sudden disappearance sent me into a mad frenzy. I looked everywhere for her. I travelled back along the roads and villages we had visited in the last year, but she was nowhere to be found. Miranda knew better than anyone how to hide. She had taught me well the art of witchcraft, of using herbs for medicine, especially how to hide more effectively from my brother. So it wasn't long before I gave up my search. She would not be found if she didn't want to be.

I couldn't understand why she had left. Maybe she had thought that I had nothing more to learn from her now. Or maybe she was just bored of caring for me. It was hard to know. I had thought she loved me. I wept at night, hoping she would return and say, 'This is another lesson you must learn.' Maybe it was a lesson. I had to rely solely on myself, for mortals were fickle and their lives too limited to hold onto. Sometimes at night I would dream that Miranda had been sick and had wished to spare me the pain of her death. I never learnt the truth and it was an ache that throbbed in my heart for centuries.

I travelled for years. Lovers and food came and went and then, to my surprise, I felt another overwhelming urge. When all other needs were fulfilled, I had a craving for company. I had dipped in and out of society as I travelled but I remained always on the periphery, avoiding long-term contact with others. I felt cold to humanity, despite my ability to heal them. Instead, my isolation made me selfish. I fed my desires. I did not care how I used my victims.

I joined the court of the Medici in Florence, back in Italy, at the end of the century. This world was a whirlwind of beauty that was as corrupt as any other. It was fun for a while for me to consider the seduction of someone important. I fantasised about the death of the Duke, who was known for his sexual perversity. I arrived as a Countess. For the first time in years I used my real name. I felt invulnerable.

The Florentines were welcoming. My obvious wealth, always so easy to accumulate, bought me access to all of the aristocratic homes. I had the latest Parisian fashion in my trunks and the ladies at the court, always looking for a new style or whim took to emulating some of my designs.

'Who is that?' asked the Duke as he glanced across the gardens and saw me seated beside one of the many water features.

'Countess Borgia, your highness. She is a widow of considerable equity.'

'She pleases our eye,' the Duke answered. 'Seat her near me at dinner this evening.'

I smiled to myself as I stood pretending to smell the flowers nearby. He had no way of knowing that I could hear his whispered words. The Duke moved on, but I soon became his mistress and planned the day I would kill him as he fucked me. Powerful men were so easy to manipulate. So deserving of my killing kiss.

Chapter 31 - Present

Feeding Time

Lilly falls upon the girl and rips out her throat before I reach them. She is starving. Months of hunger and disrupted feeding has made us both desperate. Tonight we behave like animals. I fall on the girl's arm, tearing the vein open and gulping down the blood. Power rushes back into my limbs as I swallow her life force. I glance up at Lilly and watch with fascination as she feeds. Gone is the time when we would play with our victims. There is no sexual satisfaction, just a meal. This is what being a vampire really means.

Too long I have been absorbed in the romance of my condition. I am no hero of paranormal fiction. I am a killer by nature. Though it is certainly true that I can be part of society if I so choose.

I resume my meal. The girl's body jerks beneath my vicious grasp. She is still alive, but is rapidly going into shock. It doesn't matter; though, our intention was to finish her completely.

Lilly sits back, licking the spillage from her hands. I feel the sexual energy returning as I look at her while gulping down the last dregs of blood from the dying teenager.

'Shame. She was only young.' But Lilly doesn't look regretful.

'She was a slut.'

'Oh yes. I never understood how girls can go out half-dressed in winter. And she came onto you in that club.'

'Were you jealous?' I ask, smiling at her. She stands up, smoothes her hands down her dress which is splattered with the girl's blood.

'Well, let's say, when she offered to give you a blowjob in the toilets in exchange for a line of heroin, and then grabbed your cock, I was not best pleased.'

Lilly holds out a hand and I take it, jumping to my feet. For the first time in weeks I am nearly back to full strength. The almost nightly encounters with the entity have left us both drained and weak. We needed blood, and quickly. The problem with this, of course, was that every time we picked a victim, the creature took it from us. It was as though it was deliberately weakening us.

Lilly had the answer.

'Let's go dancing,' she had said earlier.

A club was the perfect place to fulfil our needs. It was obvious we had to act immediately and feed.

'We need more,' Lilly says as we leave the girl hidden in a large bin in the back alley behind the club.

'Ok. But let's not specify. This seems to be working.'

We had not sensed the entity since our last encounter on the roads outside Manchester. Even so, we remained cautious. Lilly was less weakened than I, but then it seemed that the entity was focusing his energy on me. He obviously thought I was the biggest threat. We had not voiced what we both suspected, which was that the creature may be the only being on Earth that could actually destroy us.

Soaring into the air I am relieved to feel more like myself. We float, holding hands above the city. We are in Chester. It is full of quaint older buildings. The hotel we are staying in is opposite the train station and is suitably ostentatious. It fulfils my needs, though Lilly is far less fussy than I. The hotel staff whisper amongst themselves that it is haunted, but for the most part our time here has been undisturbed. I see the train station from the air and fly in that direction.

We move around slowly, looking for a likely target. A mother leaves the station leading her small child by the hand straight to an idling car. An old lady pushes her Zimmer frame down the street. A vagrant walks towards a bench at the front of the station, obviously looking for a resting place for the night. Without thinking I swoop down, picking the vagrant up off his feet and up into the air with us. His smell assaults my nostrils. He reeks of urine, faeces and BO. He is not the type of meal we would usually enjoy, but at the moment our world is on shaky ground. We cannot afford to be choosy.

I gag the man with my hand as we pull him through the window of our room. Lilly closes the window behind us and then opens the bathroom door. I pull his shocked and frightened body inside throwing him roughly into the shower. We turn on the water, rinsing him. It feels as though we are washing and preparing a meal.

'We are,' Lilly laughs. 'There's no way I'm biting him till he's clean.'

The tramp stares at her uncomprehendingly, moans and complains in a scared, quiet voice. I strip him of his ripped, worn coat and begin to peel away the remainder of his stinking clothing. Once naked, we scrub his shrivelled body under the hot water.

'Would you like some whisky?' Lilly asks, kindly. 'It must be awful being out on such a cold night.'

The tramp's cataract-impeded vision clouds up, tears fill his pale eyes. 'Are you an angel?' he asks through a mouth of missing teeth.

Lilly smiles at him. 'If it helps, yes.'

I watch her wrap a towel around him and hand him a full tumbler of whisky, which he gulps down gratefully. Lilly, my seraph, my beauty, is a cold-blooded angel of mercy. She appears outwardly to have empathy with the man. She rubs his hair dry with a hand towel. Her expression is kind when facing him, blank and cold when he can't see her. Then she feeds him glass after glass of the whisky until he begins slurring his words.

She leads him to the chair beside the bed, sitting him down and handing him a renewed glass. He is now wrapped in the thick towelling bathrobe that is complimentary to clients in our expensive suite.

'You first,' Lilly says.

'I can wait...'

'No, you're still weak. Please, darling. I want to see you back to full strength.'

I take the tramp without further thought. The skin on his throat is tough and weather-worn but my fangs break through easily. His blood erupts like a geyser, flooding my mouth. I taste the whisky, but it has no other effect than to tickle the back of my throat as his strength fills my veins. My power and vitality soar.

Lilly joins me a few minutes later, sucking on the wound I've created. We then take turns. I can taste her sweet saliva mingled with the sharper tasting blood as we drain the vagrant of every last drop he has to give.

After, when he lays dead and cooling in the chair, Lilly gazes down at his face. He looks peaceful.

'Maybe I am an Angel of Death,' she says, and I don't doubt it.

The Haunting Past

Lucrezia smiles at Lilly and I as she places her coffee cup down beside her. 'I was the Duke's mistress for a year before I saw Gabriele in Florence. I remember he had the most beautiful voice. It was your debut, I believe.' She turns to me.

'I remember.'

My mind goes back to the night I first sang, the night when I found my cousin Francesca with her lover in one of the reception rooms. 'I tried to follow you.'

'I know,' she laughs. 'In those days, that happened a lot to me.'

Lilly looks from one to the other of us. Her expression is inscrutable, and I wonder if my darling is feeling a little jealous.

'Gabriele was so beautiful, and so young. As he sang my fangs extended in pleasure and I had to hide them behind my fan until I could manage to get my lust in check,' Luci explains to Lilly.

'I can understand that,' Lilly smiles. 'He is pretty buff.'

'I was so cruel to you,' Lucrezia says suddenly, looking into my eyes. 'I'm sorry.'

'Never mind all that,' I say quickly. 'What happened next, after Florence and Venice?'

Even this brief reference reminds me of my haunting past. The pain from loss of all I had loved in my mortal life was too much to bear. I did not want to remember how we met again ten years later in Venice. Nor how she seduced me in the Doge's Palace. I couldn't revisit all that had happened after my re-birth. It would bring about too many of the most torturous memories, particularly of the death of my son, Gabi, and the lonely years that followed.

Lucrezia's face clouds over. A new fear bleeds into her eyes.

'I'm not sure what you need to know. But after you ... after Venice, nothing eventful happened. I just existed. Went from one court to the other. Enjoyed the life for a while, as well as the powerful men. They were so easy to seduce. It didn't matter how beautiful their original mistresses were. In the end I grew bored and I began to live the life of a recluse once more.'

I stir sugar into my coffee as I listen to her speak. Her lyrical voice makes the years that have passed seem so very casual and normal. This is an immortal's life passing by without incident; except, of course, for the daily routine of murder and the constant craving for blood, which ultimately drives and motivates all of our actions.

Lucrezia brushes her blonde curls from her eyes as Lilly nods sympathetically to her story. I am not zoned out. I scan Lucrezia's words for information. As always I am very aware of Lilly's heightened energy, as it flows around and through me. I stroke her leg under the table subconsciously. It is almost as though I cannot be near her without touching her, as if I still cannot believe she is really mine.

'And nothing significant happened?' Lilly asks, sounding surprised. 'You never found Miranda?'

'No. And as the years passed I gave up hope of seeing her again. I knew she must have died. When I'd known her she was in her early twenties, though she seemed to have the experience of old age. And as I reached my two hundredth birthday, I knew there was no point in even considering that anyone from my old life still existed, save perhaps Caesare. But I still thought of her and I still dreamt of the day she saved me. Other than that, nothing of note happened. At least not until Paris many years later.'

Chapter 33 - Lucrezia's Story
The Haunting Past

'He's coming. Run, Luci.'

I felt the wind rushing through my hair as I was swept up from my bed and out through the open window into the night sky long before I could become fully lucid. The white lace hem of my nightgown caught on the edge of the balcony, tearing loudly as my captor refused to pause. The translucent fibres were visible in the candlelight as the tiny threads snapped and sprayed into the air in a cloud of dust, reflected by the light shining from the moon.

I had been ripped from my sleep yet it lingered still, numbed my senses. I couldn't open my eyes, and my head lolled over the arm of my captor like a rag doll carried by a spoilt child..

It was Caesare, of course. But Caesare was no adolescent. He was a man. No, he was more than that; he was an immortal, and that was far more dangerous. I tried to shake myself out of the dream. Miranda had appeared so often in my thoughts lately, and now I knew why. Some instinct had warned me of Caesare; somehow he had penetrated my protection spells. Then, he had two hundred years to learn how.

We ascended through the cold sky. The freezing Paris fog whipped over my now bare legs as we rose up and above it. There was no respite from the cold, even though I knew – had known for a long time – that the cold could not hurt me, that I couldn't be easily killed. Nevertheless, extreme conditions could be uncomfortable and even painful. My face, hands and feet stung with the frost. My dull eyes tried to pick out light from the windows of bars and restaurants; any signs of life below. The freezing fog was too dense and distorted the buildings, warping them into unrecognisable phantoms.

We travelled through the night. My limbs we numb, my faculties dimmed, often I cried out in pain at the relentlessness of Caesare's flight.

'Please,' I begged. 'Caesare! No ...'

My face was buffeted by the wind. Though I could barely see my brother through my half closed eyes, I noticed for the first time that he had shaved away the facial hair that for most of his life had been his trademark. His teeth were gritted, his jaw set into a harsh line. His eyes, peering out from under the brim of a hat firmly placed on his head, pierced the night like green beacons. His silence was more terrifying than any of his old threats had ever been. I was held immobile with his arms braced around my waist.

A violent cascade of fear engulfed my heart. Every muscle in my body ached. I drifted in and out of consciousness. If I had been mortal, I would have died for certain in the first hour.

Horror and panic swam with the fresh blood I'd consumed that evening, swirling around my stomach in a nauseous mass. He had found me. How on earth had I thought to escape him?

Caesare was stronger, more powerful than I remembered. His arms felt like forged metal as I struggled against him. My efforts had little more effect than the punches of a child in the throes of a tantrum. As I hit out he barely shrugged to subdue me and I tired quickly. I realised I must be victim to some wicked spell because my body felt so weak and limp against his strength when physically we should have been evenly matched.

The night stretched into early morning. I could see the sun rising over the snowy peaks of the Alps. At the sight of this distant, rising inferno Caesare gasped and we abruptly plummeted thousands of feet towards the ground. I shrieked in fear, not knowing whether the impact from such a height could kill us both. The roar of the wind in my ears deafened me as we fell down and down and the hard, snow-packed earth grew closer to my horrified eyes. I tore at his thick, black, velvet frock coat trying to break free, but he pulled me closer to his chest. Even though I pushed against him with all my remaining strength, I was helpless as we headed down, gaining momentum. I closed my eyes, bracing my body for the collision.

Caesare halted in mid-air. We were thirty or forty feet from the ground. The sudden stop jerked my body agonisingly. My head hit his shoulder with a concussing blow. I grunted and flopped against him. He held me for a moment. I felt him push my hair, a knotted mass, away from my fear-frozen cheeks with uncharacteristic tenderness. Confused, I opened my eyes and saw that his own eyes burned with a new, unfamiliar light. My heart thumped as he scrutinised me.

We headed down further and arrived in the midst of a dense forest. Caesare flipped me effortlessly in his arms, like a groom carrying his bride; running with me, gliding easily through the trees.

'Are you insane?' I gasped when I was able to speak again.

His laughter roared and a flock of birds screeched up into the air in fright.

'Please stop! I can walk for myself.'

'No. We need to make my lair before the dawn fully breaks.'

'Why?'

He ran faster. He was quicker, more agile than I had ever been. I realised with fear, as I looked up into his face, that the vampiric infection was different with him. It was far darker, more intensely evil. I knew then the answer to my question. The superstitious belief held by peasants was that vampires had to shun the daylight, yet this had never been the case for me. Somehow Caesare had evolved and now he fulfilled the common belief. The sun was painful, possibly even deadly, to him.

The dawn began to filter through the trees. Caesare stumbled, smashing our bodies against the hard wood of an oak as he sought cover; but my body was numb now and I no longer felt pain. When an occasionally sliver of light landed on him he howled like an injured wolf. But always he ran, keeping to the shadows as best he could. His grip also tightened around me. I knew that escape was completely impossible.

The trees thinned. Gaining shelter from the warming sun became increasingly hard for him to achieve. He flitted from shadow to shadow. His hold on me loosened as he became more distracted. I began to hope that maybe I could break free of him. No sooner had the thought drifted through my mind than a drug-like drowsiness anaesthetized me again. Caesare had been exerting some supernatural will over me. He was using the last of his strength to retain his control. I fought the swoon that threatened to engulf me. The snow-covered trees blurred into a swirl of brown and white that no longer made any sense to my repressed senses.

Ahead loomed the most prevalent, darkest shadow yet. As the forest dwindled we came upon an opening that led directly into the mountainside. With a last spurt of energy Caesare broke free of the remaining tree cover. His eyes were now red balls of bleeding fire. I felt his skin quickly warm and ignite as he headed through the sunlight.

Chapter 34 - Lucrezia's Story

False Security

I woke to the sound of running water. My eyes were hazy, crusted with grime from the journey. My limbs felt stiff and sore. Under my body I felt the soft texture of pure silk spread over a yielding mattress. My fingers twitched with pins and needles as feeling began to return to them. I lifted my hand and looked at it stupidly; it felt as though it didn't belong to me. I forced it to move and tried to rub my eyes. My nails were torn and thick with dirt as though I had tried to claw my way out of the grave.

'In a way you did,' a voice murmured softly from somewhere above me.

Memory returned in a rush and I tried to sit up, collapsing back as dizziness overtook me. Caesare. Oh my God! He could still read my thoughts.

He chuckled. A tremor shuddered through my body.

'Of course, Luci. I always could.'

I focused my eyes above me, expecting to see him towering there. Nothing. I tried to move my head, but my neck was immobile. Panic gripped my mind. I was paralysed, helpless. Maybe I had been injured irreparably during the journey? Crippled in some way? My other hand flew to my throat. I gasped for air, suffocating on my own fear as I pawed at my skin. There was an invisible force that seemed to hold me flat against the bed.

'Be still,' he said. 'Your strength will return soon. I had to use a spell on you. It will take time to wear off.'

So. He knew about spells and magic. Why was I surprised?

'Where am I?' I croaked. 'You have no right ...'

'You belong to me.' His voice was definite, matter-of-fact.

White hot tears leaked from my eyes and slid down my temples to merge with the grit in my hair. I shook my head in denial. Relief rushed into my face in a hot flush when I realised I had movement at last. Slowly my limbs began to twitch back to life and I felt less powerless. Within a few minutes my eyesight sharpened and I could see the ceiling of the room more clearly. It was draped in purple silk that scooped down and up in the style of a luxurious Arab tent. I turned my head slowly, expecting discomfort or pain but felt neither as it moved freely.

My eyes scanned the room. The wall to my far left was covered in a bright tapestry. Woven in rich, warm colours, it depicted the scene of a masked ball. I was fascinated, even mesmerised by the vibrantly dressed revellers, as they stood poised with their dance partners. Around the dancers, a group of musicians with intense expressions played their instruments. Chamber music came to my ears. The figures on the tapestry moved, swirling and sweeping as the music grew louder, faster. I struggled for breath, my pulse racing in time with the melody. I closed my eyes and the music faded. I looked once more at the tapestry and immediately heard the angelic tones of a harp. Confused, I turned away. The music faded again to a distant echo. I lay, my hands covering my closed eyes, until the room steadied and only silence remained.

When I opened my eyes again I found myself looking at an ornate fireplace that seemed to be carved from rock rather than marble. Caesare stood, one elbow resting on the mantelpiece as he gazed into the flames. He was dressed in black, just as he had been when he tore me from my bed. He wore a black ruffled shirt, loosely over tight leather breeches. Only now he no longer wore the velvet frock coat and brimmed hat that had been pulled down over his brow to shelter him from the sun. Beautiful, elegant, slender, feline, even down to the long tapered fingers that rested on his face, my brother was indeed a handsome man. His beardless face looked younger and fresher than I recalled. In the firelight his skin glowed with that same translucent whiteness as my own. His hair, the same white gold as mine, was pulled back into a tail that was tied neatly by a leather thong. I admired his profile. Sharper, crueller than mine, but the family resemblance was so acute that I almost felt I was seeing myself dressed as a man.

He seemed lost in thought, or maybe he merely enjoyed my scrutiny. I wasn't sure, but I pulled my eyes away from his hypnotic frame and looked around the room.

I found I could sit as I pushed up against the downy mattress. I shuffled upwards, resting my back against an ornate headboard that was covered with carved cherubs. Its design matched the furniture in the room. There was a writing bureau, open with a piece of parchment lying flat next to an inkpot and quill.

At the bottom of the bed there was a wardrobe; beautiful carvings swirled around the fine mirrors that covered the doors. A shivering, bedraggled wreck sat wide eyed in the bed. With shock I realised it was my own reflection. I looked like a mad woman deserted at the gates of an asylum. My nightgown was filthy and torn and hung from my shoulders like paupers' rags. I closed my eyes to the horror of myself and flopped back against the comfort of the pillows.

A dressing table sat under what I assumed was a curtained window. A large heart-shaped mirror pivoted on a frame made from the same wood above pots of creams and cosmetics that I recognised as the type I used. I felt disorientated. My head was thick with confusion.

'For you.'

From the corner of my eye I saw Caesare sweep his arm out around the room.

'What do you mean "for me"?'

'I hope you aren't going to be ungrateful, Lucrezia.'

His face was turned to me as he now sat casually on the edge of the bed. I started at his nearness. I had been unaware of his movement and a new fear surged through me as I wondered if I had lost my supernatural instincts. My brother had always had power over me, long before he learnt what real power was. But I was no longer a frightened teenage girl under his abusive sway. Although I had sorcery of my own to call on, I would wait until the time was right to use it.

'I made it for you. For your comfort,' he answered.

I was stunned into silence. He'd always planned to reclaim me; my freedom and the past two hundred years meant nothing at all. So typical of Caesare. I suspected he'd been playing his games all this time, allowing me freedom only to snatch it away when I was fully lulled into a false sense of security.

'Where am I?' I asked again.

'Somewhere safe.'

He smiled. I curled up in terror at the predatory gleam in his green eyes. His fangs glowed in the dim light, matching the shine of his eyes.

'The bathroom is through that door, my dear,' he said, pointing to my right at an alcove I hadn't noticed. 'I'm sure you'll want to clean up before dinner.'

'Dinner?'

'Of course. You must be hungry.'

'Are we... to be so civilised then?'

'Luci, what do you take me for? A barbarian?' With that he stood and left the room. I barely registered the whoosh of another curtain as it raised, briefly uncovering a doorway before it fell flat back in place as though it had never been disturbed.

The room was bewitched. I knew that it was entirely useless to even consider escape until I understood what kind of sorcery was in play. Miranda had taught me to recognise and break wards, and the key to this was in understanding the elements that held the spell together. So for now, Caesare had me again, and this time he would not let me go without a fight. I gathered my senses and my talents and began to weave a seeking spell, which would reveal all points of magic in my surroundings.

I may have been trapped, but I was not helpless.

Chapter 35 - Lucrezia's Story

Enchanted Waterfall

The bathroom was large and surprisingly warm even though the floor was made from beige marble. Hot water sluiced like a natural waterfall from a hole in the wall into a sunken pool that was big enough to swim in. A thick robe, in luxurious taffeta and lace, lay over an upright wooden chair that matched the furnishing in the bedroom.

Above the entrance to the room, two carved stone cherubs leered at me as I undressed. I dropped my filthy, shredded clothing to the floor and stepped into the water. The pool was deep, carved with grooves around the sides which served as seating and steps. I sat in a corner beside a gold dish that held sweetly perfumed soap. The water was the perfect temperature. Its warmth flooded my skin, reminding me of just how cold my body had been from both the flight and the hours of immobility. I wondered, not for the first time, what power my brother must now wield that he could incapacitate me by the sheer force of his mind.

I wiped away my fears and phobias as I washed myself, feeling vampiric strength and power return to my muscles as I lathered my skin and hair. The soap dripped from my skin into the pool where it disappeared leaving the liquid clean and clear. It was obvious that the whole place was redolent with sorcery.

Once clean, I swam, feeling the silken fluid relax my muscles as I floated and rolled, enjoying the fresh sensation of the pure, hot water. I lost sense of time and place again. I felt like a nymph frolicking in the pool of some unknown god in a magical forest. It felt like something out of the pagan world of innocence when the Goddess and her God roamed the world. My mind flashed back to Miranda's stories.

Foliage sprouted up through the marble. I smelt the fresh scent of pine, exotic flowers, and the tang of dew dripping from dark green leaves. The torrent of hot water from the wall became a real waterfall, churning the liquid in the pool. It tugged at my limbs as a fierce current built up underneath the surface.

Invisible fingers swirled around my breasts, invaded the space between my legs, touching and caressing. I pushed away and swam towards the side. The waterfall became fiercer, more demanding, swirls and eddies of water rushed around me, forcing my legs apart. I was dragged under, held there by an unspecific force. I battled against the water, gagging and choking as I fought my way back to the surface. There I found the forest receding and the stark marble tiles of the bathroom becoming visible once more.

I stumbled from the pool, reaching for the robe as the echo of cruel laughter drowned out the steady drum of the water. I crumpled to the floor on my hands and knees, hacking water from my lungs. I couldn't drown, but the water hurt nonetheless. It was a relief to drain my chest of its last invasive presence.

'Stop it, damn you!' I called to the unresponsive walls.

I swallowed, calming myself. Caesare's games had always petrified me but now I was much harder to hurt. I too was immortal, and I was determined that if he could not destroy my body then he would never crush my spirit.

I pulled the clean taffeta over my still wet body and tied the robe tightly around my waist. I walked back into the bedchamber and the fabric stained in patches as the damp seeped from my skin. The marble floor was warm under my bare feet. Heat poured from the walls; the temperature was like a tropical greenhouse. It was hard to imagine the snow I'd seen, outside, as we arrived.

I noted that while I had been bathing, the bed had been remade and a gown of bright red silk lay across it. Next to the gown laid a chemise, a corset, stockings and some pantaloons in crisp white cotton. I smiled coldly at the irony of this formal clothing with all the appropriate trappings that a lady of quality needed to be respectable. Then I reached for a pale pink towel that was folded on the chair beside the bed. Removing the robe I dried myself thoroughly.

'Well, you haven't lost your sense of humour,' I said calmly as I dressed. 'You want games? All right! I can play them too.'

I expected laughter, the essence of his mockery seeping through the stone, but a disconcerting silence greeted me. As I pulled on the silk stockings, fastened them with soft red garters, my emotions wavered between insecurity and empowerment. I was heartened by the knowledge that I'd survived his cruelty once before. I could do it again. What on earth could Caesare do to me now that he had not already done? Of course I knew more now, had in fact my own witchcraft to call on. But for now, that would remain untested. I did not wish to reveal my hand too soon.

Feeling composed, I made my way to the curtained doorway through which Caesare had made his exit. As I drew nearer, the curtain flew open and the doorway was revealed. It was an oval arch carved out of rock. Was his lair really cut deep into the mountain? If so, what would I find beyond the archway?

For a moment I paused. The chamber seemed like a haven to me suddenly. It was familiar and warm. What lay in wait beyond the arch could mean danger, pain and cruelty. I shivered. Fear seemed so ridiculous. I had survived being burnt at the stake … nothing could kill me! A subtle breeze and the smell of fresh air wafted into the room. I drank it. Breathed it. It tasted of freedom and propelled me forward out into the darkness beyond.

I found myself in a long corridor carved out of the rock. As I walked forward, torches set in freestanding holders along the walls to either side burst alight to guide my progress. The gentle breeze pushed at the flames and the fire shadows glimmered up against the walls. The torches looked like soldiers standing impatiently to attention. As I passed them they flickered out as though someone had used a giant snuff. They were merely candles extinguished when their light was no longer needed.

I reached the doorway at the end in a few seconds and it swung open in greeting before me. Again I paused on the threshold. My breath, held subconsciously, huffed out as light burst into being beyond the door. I stepped forward ready to face anything and everything.

Beyond I found a huge dining room. An excessively large table reached from one end of the room to the other. In the centre of the room was a huge open fireplace, with marble pews curved around the fire. The room was dimly lit, with only a few candelabras standing on the table, which was set with only two places, exactly in the centre of the table facing each other. The place settings were made of pure gold and reflected the light from the fire.

'I thought you might feel less intimidated with the table between us as we eat. Though I'm sure you know I would rather be much closer to you, Luci.'

I swallowed and looked to where Caesare was slouched in an armchair at the far end of the room, one booted foot resting on a leather footstool. He held a crystal glass in his hand, which looked as though it contained claret. Beside him was a small round table that held a crystal decanter and another glass on a silver tray.

'You're right. I would prefer some distance between us ... Preferably thousands of miles,' I snapped.

He sat forward in his chair. His foot slammed to the floor and he raised his glass as though he would hurl it at me for my insolence. I raised my chin and glared at him. Damn him! I wouldn't back down, even if he crushed every bone in my body! He stared at me for a moment, before lifting the glass in the air as though in salute. Then he swigged ungracefully, downing the contents in a single gulp.

'You always bait me,' he laughed. 'Would you like some of this rather fine claret, Lucrezia?'

I blinked. Had I won some minor victory?

'You are the very picture of propriety, brother dearest.' I sneered.

'You'll find me much changed.'

I didn't answer, but I doubted his new found self-control would last beyond the first hour.

'Please, sit. You must be famished; you've slept for three days.'

'What?'

I walked to the table and allowed Caesare to push the seat gently under me like the gentleman I knew he wasn't. My brother was seated opposite me before I had even spread my napkin over my knee.

A feeling of unreality overtook me once more as a tiny unspeaking servant in a black monk-like robe served us with a steaming bowl of thick soup. I was offered a platter of fresh, warm bread. I ate, at first by instinct, but soon the broth revived me. I found myself swirling my gold spoon over the empty bottom of the bowl. The servant reappeared to remove the dishes, followed by a second waiter, a clone of the first, who placed a plate of carved chicken breast in a fruity sauce where the bowl had been. I ate the succulent meat and realised I was actually starving. It was only when I had finished that I noticed my brother watching me intently. He had barely touched his own food. Instead he had continued to fill his wine glass from the decanter he'd brought to the table.

I picked up my own glass and sipped at the full-bodied fruity red wine. It slithered deliciously around my tongue and warmed my throat as I swallowed. I knew that I could not become intoxicated yet there was always a slight thrill when I drank a good, strong wine, a minor rush of blood to my brain. Then my body fought off the effects.

'I've always enjoyed watching you eat.' Caesare smiled companionably.

I swallowed again. His scrutiny made me feel uncomfortable. He reached once more for the decanter, removed the stopper and poured the wine slowly into his glass. In the old days, watching him drink this much, I would have become anxious. My brother became crueller when he drank. Now I knew that, like me, the alcohol would have no effect on him at all. This thought was even more terrifying.

I waited as he swirled his drink casually in his hand. His eyes seemed to pierce the bottom of the glass as he looked deeply into it like a fortune-teller reading a crystal ball. I dabbed my lips with the napkin. I felt revived, back to full strength. I realised that unless I learnt to allay the effect, Caesare could subdue me with his spells at anytime. I reached for my glass once more and my brother fell from his trance to look up at me. He watched me sip lightly at the wine. His eyes traced the flick of my tongue as I licked my lips to remove traces of the liquid. His gaze narrowed. I pulled my napkin up to my mouth again in a reflex gesture that was more than self-conscious.

His eyes changed from green to red in a blink. I felt his lust powerfully transmitted to me, overwhelming my aura, suffocating my psyche. I gasped for air, as passion soared through my blood in response to his power. Caesare towered over. My head threw back with a will of its own as I lolled in the chair like a drunken whore displaying her wares for a customer. His hands worked at the bodice; sharp nails shredded the fabric as if it were paper.

My breasts spilled from my chemise into his warm hands as I watched him through lust-filled eyes. My body ached with desire as I saw his fangs lengthen. His mouth lowered to my white flesh, teeth grazing the skin until I squirmed with yearning. He reared his head a little, teasing my nipple with the tip of his tongue.

I felt my own fangs emerge from their sheaths in response, the blood throbbing through my gums making me dizzy.

Don't let him bite you. Miranda's familiar voice echoed in my head pushing back the lust spell.

'No!' I gasped.

He chuckled deep in his throat.

'You want me, my dear, as much as I desire you.'

'No.' I pushed away, throwing my chair backwards while ripping myself from his grasp. 'I will never willingly let you touch me. You'll have to kill me, Caesare! You'll have to kill me! Do you understand?'

I raced across the room, past where he had sat by the fireplace, and ran full pelt towards a door, which was half covered with another tapestry. An invisible force physically wrenched me backwards. I slammed painfully against the table.

My breath huffed out from me. I lay for a moment stunned on the floor. Caesare stood above me. As I looked up the back of his hand whipped down and slammed against my cheek, fracturing bone and throwing me hard back against the stone floor. Blood burst from my nose and I felt my flesh rip where I'd been struck. A momentary pain surged through my face and nose. Red fluid, my life force, poured from the wound briefly before flesh and bone knitted back together repairing itself with barely an ache.

He reached for me again, lifting my struggling body above his head, before throwing me roughly onto the dinner table, scattering the settings, which clashed and clattered across the floor. Then his arms pinned me down as he glared closely into my face. I cried out with shock. His features were feral. His bottom lip bled where his fangs repeatedly bit into it.

'Damn you! Let me go!' I cried.

As if my words held power, invisible hands caught him. They pulled him roughly away from my trembling body.

It was then I saw them. Tiny people! All around the room they appeared, as if from nowhere. They never moved. The whites of their eyes exposed their presence as they blinked in unison. I tried to focus on them, to see their features more clearly, but once again the darkness took me.

The Impossible Garden

When I opened my eyes I was in a garden.

It was not only beautiful but also enchanted. It stretched for miles around me, and although it was as bright as any sunny day, I could see that there was no natural sky above. The most stunning foliage grew directly from the rock, as though it were the most fertile of soil. Yet we were still underground. The garden was built beneath thousands of feet of rock, right in the heart of the mountain.

I was lying on a patch of grass. A beautiful, refreshing breeze wafted warm and comforting through the blades of grass and across my cheek, fooling me briefly into believing there was a passageway to the outside somewhere in this underground world.

I thought for a moment that I was dreaming. It was as if I had been freed and was outside once more, away from the terror of my childhood. But no, the garden was all a part of this massive illusion. Or so I believed.

People were there. I was aware of them, smelt their blood as they worked and sweated among the plants. They grew food in one area. Fruits I'd never seen before, and some that resembled apples, peaches and grapes but which perhaps were something entirely different.

The sheer impossibility of the existence of this place staggered me. I sat up on the grass, only to find a bench grow beneath me. Shaping itself from rock it turned into wood that formed around me for my comfort. A huge vine-covered arch grew from its side, swooping in a curve above my head.

'I'm insane. You've driven me mad, Caesare,' I murmured and he laughed.

'This place is amazing, I agree. But all that you see is real.'

'It's impossible. An impossible garden.'

'Yes. In the world you know but then we are impossible too, aren't we?'

'I can't take in what I see. What is this place?'

It was the ultimate sorcery. My years with Miranda had taught me nothing compared to this mysterious power. If the people of this world used this magic to find me for him, then it was no surprise that my defences were as weak as a house of cards.

Caesare grew quiet. He picked a flower from its stalk and immediately it was replaced on the plant by a tiny bud that slowly blossomed. He handed me the flower. A somewhat awkward expression tweaked his lips into a half smile.

'This place is another world, Luci. These people another race. And their laws and beliefs are far different from the ones imposed by Christianity and the Vatican.'

'Who are they?'

'They call themselves the Allucians. They are an ancient and powerful race. Their abilities stretch beyond the realms of our known world.'

I looked around as the people, formerly hidden from my sight, emerged on cue. They were olive-skinned and delicate; a race of tiny people. A child approached, and her miniature hand stretched out to offer me what appeared to be an orange. Her size belied her age. In height, she appeared no older than a three year old, but her features and proportions implied that in development she was possibly ten or twelve years old. Her delicate bones and characteristics were doll-like. Never had I seen skin and hair that shone with such polished lustre. She was beautiful. To my shame, I felt a pang of hunger.

She kneeled before me and I took the fruit, peeling it to reveal flesh of a peach-like texture. I bit into it and my mouth was filled with fresh, warm blood – the sweetest most delicious food source I had ever tasted.

'They always give you what you need. You were weakened, Luci.'

I swooned, could almost taste and hear the heartbeat of a kill, felt filled beyond capacity. I zoned out, lost sense of time, floated on the bench, the blood sweet and pure on my lips, in my mouth and in my stomach.

Then Caesare was seated beside me. The bench was now part of a boat that glided on a river through the garden. His lips kissed mine, sharing the taste of blood. His arousal was evident as his lips possessed me with his usual fanatical passion.

Miranda's face flashed before my eyes.

'Luci!' she cried with her old, familiar frustration. 'Wake up!'

The spell broke. I found that my bodice was open, my pale breasts cupped by Caesare's hands. He was kissing my throat. I pushed him away.

'I hate you!'

'They always give me what I need,' he said again. The realisation that I was what he needed, or wanted, floated to the surface of my befuddled mind, making me aware that I had no chance of escaping this place, these people. They were too powerful.

Caesare's laughter shook me.

'Oh, Luci, of course you can't escape. They want my happiness. They gave you back to me! The one woman I have always desired.'

'What do you mean they gave me back to you?'

'Not now,' he replied, drooping his hand to trail in the clear water.

'Caesare. We are brother and sister. Your infatuation with me was always a sin. You raped me when I fifteen! I loved you once and you hurt me. Since then I have never been willing. How can this be acceptable in their world? In any world?'

'Their laws, as I explained, are different. Sometimes, brother and sister do consort in their society.'

I grew silent. Thinking hard. How could I gain some advantage?

'You said they always give you what you want? Well I want my freedom!'

'Freedom?' He laughed. 'Well you will have that, Luci. You are free to go anywhere within the mountain, of course.'

'But ...'

'Don't try to fight this. I am their God. My needs will always supersede yours. After that, every effort will be made to ensure you are as comfortable and happy as possible.'

'Happy? I'm a prisoner! And I will never willingly let you touch me!'

Caesare smiled with the surety of a man used to getting his own way. His expression chilled me. The boat followed the river deeper into the garden, carried along by the gentle breeze.

Here and there I spied the Allucians weeding and tending the food sources. I was oddly emotionless. I felt no fear or distress, only a clear understanding of the situation. I would have to bide my time. I was certain that I would find my way out of this supernatural maze; that once again, I would escape my possessive brother. I searched for the magic incantations that Miranda had given me last of all, but my memory failed me. I was unable to recall my words of power, words that would have blasted a hole right through the rock to the outside world. I cursed myself for the complacency that had led me to stop using the magic several years before. Lack of use had made me forget my power. Or maybe this place dampened it. Other than my usual strength I seemed unable to achieve even the smallest spell.

The boat slid gently into a small jetty. Here Caesare disembarked and turned to me. He stretched out a hand. I ignored him and leaped from the boat to the land myself.

At that moment an adult Allucian stepped forward from behind a beautiful bush, which was in full bloom with peach coloured flowers. She was the most stunning creature I'd ever seen. Her skin shone with a golden hue, her black hair was reflected moonlight in the fake sun. Behind her was an entourage of Allucians, all official in their demeanour.

She came forward and bowed her head, palms together, submissively acknowledging Caesare. As I turned to look at him I noticed he returned her bow with equal respect.

'Princess Ilura, this is Lucrezia,' Caesare introduced us with the formality of the Papal court.

Clearly Ilura was important, and the minute her eyes met mine, I knew my presence here did not please her. Though I didn't know why.

'My father waits for you,' said Ilura. I heard her words but her lips didn't move. 'I would like to offer my companionship to Lucrezia, if you will it?'

'Of course,' Caesare replied.

He was at home completely with the telepathy of her conversation. He bowed once more to her as some private exchange, which I was excluded from, occurred between them.

'I have duties to attend to.' Caesare turned to me. 'Ilura will show you around and perhaps may make you feel more at home.'

'What duties?'

'Being a God comes with responsibilities; I will explain all in time. But for now, have a pleasant afternoon and I will see you again this evening.'

Caesare left and the foliage swallowed him as though he had never been there. Caesare with responsibilities? I shook my head and looked up. I found myself staring at Ilura. Her unreadable, calm eyes scrutinised me in return.

'So. Tell me about your people, Princess,' I said to break the stillness and silence between us.

'What do you wish to know?' Her voice echoed in my head, leaving me with the sensation of unreality.

'I want to know how you can justify keeping me prisoner.'

Immediately, Ilura's passive face broke into a full smile.

'Ah. Now that … is a very long story. But not one easily told.'

I looked at her. 'Well, I don't seem to have anything else to do.'

'We are an Indian tribe,' she continued. 'An ancient people with many mysteries and rites that you may not, at first, understand.'

I'd heard of such tribes, seen the visions of a sailor whose blood I drank in my little rooms above the tavern in the docks. The image of an Incan society floated behind dying eyes, spilling the sight of their temple into my mind. Gold and jewels adorned the walls and pillars of this mysterious world. I had thought it was merely a dying man's fantasy of the riches he never found. Yet here, in the world of the Allucians, I found myself wondering where that mysterious bounty lay.

'Gold and jewels are easily obtainable,' Ilura said. 'But happiness is not. My tribe strives to survive, and we have for hundreds of years, though our world was dying until we found Lord Caesare.'

Startled, I looked at her. 'What positive impact could he possibly have on your world?'

Ilura said nothing. I could barely even hear the movement of the river beside us.

'I just wish to understand.'

Quietly she turned to me. A typhoon of stories and images whirled into my head. The Allucians were ancient, powerful but they were also very peaceful and they abhorred violence. Therefore, Caesare would never be allowed to hurt me. His behaviour the night before had been noted.

'We cannot allow that,' she said. 'He will not be permitted to force himself on you. So be reassured, his goal is to win back your love.'

'And if he can't?'

Ilura's expression remained closed. 'He will.'

'I'm tired,' I replied. 'I want to return to my chamber.'

In the evening Caesare stayed away. His absence, coupled with the eerie silence of the servants as they placed food before me in the dining room, made me feel increasingly nervous. It was as though I was in some luxurious prison. All my needs would be met. I would be fed, clothed, made comfortable, given everything except the one thing I wanted – my freedom.

I wandered the narrow corridors late at night, familiarising myself with the layout of my new domain, like a lion pacing his cage. It didn't matter how many times I traversed each area it remained the same. There were no windows to see the outside world, no doors to escape through, no one to talk to.

By morning I was exhausted. I stumbled my way back into the bedchamber, throwing myself onto the bed like a spoilt child. Even then sleep was a slow companion to arrive. Eventually when I drifted off it was only into a shallow slumber that was filled with vivid, violent dreams, all of my childhood.

Chapter 37 - Lucrezia's Story
The Allucian City

Six weeks later I knew every part of the mountain, even the areas that constantly changed and adapted to our needs. I realised that the garden itself rarely changed. If it did, it was as though I had merely been transported to another part of it as I wished, rather than an alteration of the main structure.

Within the mountain was a city. Here the Allucians lived, worked and died, although death among them was a rarity. I learnt from Ilura that they lived long and healthy lives.

'But, surely that could be a problem,' I said.

'Potentially,' Ilura replied. 'However, births are even rarer.'

'I see.'

'Pregnancy among our women is an honour. And has only become possible again since Lord Caesare joined us.'

'Ah. So that is his duty then?'

Ilura laughed. 'Of course not. It's only that his presence among us helps us to survive.'

'How?'

'Lord Caesare saved us,' she continued ignoring my question. 'We were a dying people.'

She was beginning to sound like a fanatic, as though these words were some kind of mantra that they all learnt by rote. Caesare saved them, they were grateful, but further explanation of how never came. I questioned her further. Ilura grew silent and thoughtful, refusing to answer no matter how much I badgered her. She smiled instead, saying all would come clear in time. From this I gathered that the Allucians considered my brother's presence a blessing and attributed their new fertility to him in some way.

Every day I spent time with Ilura. She was my only friend in an entire society of unique people. In these early weeks I saw little of Caesare during the daytime, but spent my evenings with him in the dining room, eating the delicious food provided by the Allucians. Caesare made no more attempts to seduce or coerce me into fulfilling his sexual needs, rather seemed content to just enjoy my company.

'Come,' Ilura said one afternoon. 'I want to show you something.'

We were on the river and the boat took us to a gateway entrance I had never seen before. As the gate opened, the boat transformed into a carriage led by four small horses, the river became a road. We travelled leisurely through the citadel that I had so far not been permitted to see or visit.

It was a beautiful world. Houses cut into the rock rose up either side of the streets like modern high rises made of marble; house upon house stacked too high to see the tops. They reached up into the false sky, while the underworld sun shone down on the gleaming white of the structures. The streets were clean, white pavements, white streets. It was the realised dream of heaven. Pure.

The vacuum of sound in the city was eerie. Although the streets were busy, bustling even, rarely a sound could be heard; but then, the Allucians didn't speak out loud. Their telepathy was silent unless meant for the person addressed. Occasionally they had an open sound when more people were included in the conversation. Caesare said that this only happened in social situations. At times the sound of all of them talking was, or could be, difficult to understand. It went straight into your mind and was not filtered or selective like our own hearing. It was the chatter of all of them talking at once that made it hard. Generally that never happened which made their speech patterns very different to our own. They never overlapped each other. Communication was ultimately very polite.

Free of the garden, free of the limited rooms I had been given access to, I felt suddenly light-hearted. We travelled for about half an hour, weaving in and out of street after street, each one a simulacrum of the other, until I was unsure whether this was all some elaborate illusion designed to confuse me. Then finally we drove up a curving driveway, to what seemed like nothing short of a palace.

White and imposing it reared above us like some bleached asylum. A shiver rippled down my spine. I knew I was on the cusp of some revelation.

'Where are we?' I asked.

Ilura smiled. 'The nursery.'

She took my hand and led me from the carriage. 'Don't be afraid, Lucrezia. This is what you wanted to know about us.'

The coach pulled up alongside an imposing staircase and the driver jumped down quickly and opened the door for us. I followed Ilura out of the coach and up the steps to a huge white door. As we approached, the door swung open silently and we entered the nursery.

My first perception prickled up the back of my neck: the nursery looked like a palace converted into a hospital.

'Yes,' Ilura said. 'Our nursery is a palace and a place of worship if you like. This is a very important building.'

I followed Ilura into a huge hallway, which was dominated by a daunting centre staircase. To my left and to my right I saw what appeared to be two long corridors. The corridors seemed to stretch into infinity. I thought this some other Allucian trick. On each side of each corridor was a row of doors. I couldn't study this longer as Ilura took my hand and led me up the staircase. She paused for a moment halfway up and glanced ahead as though she could hear something. Of course she could; someone was talking to her.

'The babies are excited to be having a visitor.' She smiled

finally. 'Come.' Instead of reassuring me, her smile gripped my stomach and nausea rushed into my gullet in a sickening wave.

I let her lead me all the same. With every step we took upstairs I felt the strangest sensation, as though this new revelation would inevitably mean certain doom.

At the top of the stairs Ilura paused. She seemed to need to catch her breath, though she wasn't breathing heavily. I could feel something too and I was sure it was what caused her to stop. The air was heavy. I took a moment to look around. Either side of the landing were similar corridors to those downstairs with the exception that I could see to the end of each. This made the nursery appear unbalanced. The world of the Allucians had its own rules of physical space and so I didn't worry about the strangeness too much, merely noted it as something to consider at a later date.

By now Ilura had composed herself and she turned right, still holding my hand, and pulled me towards one of the corridors. The air looked clear but it felt wrong. Walking down the corridor gave me the sensation of walking through water; my feet dragged and felt heavy. It was almost like a dream. My limbs felt weighted. Every step closer to the door at the far end made the hair stand up on the nape of my neck. I didn't want to reach the end of the corridor.

'What is that?' I asked Ilura finally.

She stopped and looked at me, a confused expression on her face.

'That sensation. Is it a spell?' I continued.

'What sensation?'

Just as quickly as it had arrived, the feeling fled. I felt almost weightless in comparison.

'It's gone,' I said.

Ilura stared at me for a moment. Her expression showed confusion yet her eyes held an element of something else. Maybe it was fear I saw skitter across her shiny pupils, but it was gone almost as soon as it had appeared.

'You didn't feel anything?' I asked.

Ilura shrugged. 'It's this way.'

The babies lay in cots in one small dormitory. There were ten in all. Not a huge number for a society of thousands of people, although an exciting prospect for them none-the-less. They were each attended by an Allucian nurse who sat beside each cot, waiting silently. The nurses were eerily still. They sat with their hands on their laps. None of them looked at us. It was as if they were in their own unique little world.

'What am I looking at?'

'The Allucians have longevity, Lucrezia.' Ilura smiled. 'Some, like my father, have lived for centuries. But this has an impact on society. No new blood has been born to our people for over a hundred years ...'

'But... Ilura, that's ridiculous, you're only a young girl. And the little girl who brought me the first day was no more than twelve.'

Ilura smiled again. 'I seem so, but I am over two hundred years old. And yes, the girl you saw has been the youngest member of our society for a very long time. But then, you understand that, Lucrezia, because you and Lord Caesare are immortal. Two hundred years is nothing to you.'

'So, you're immortal too?'

'No. This is why it is so important that we continue to procreate. We were dying, Lucrezia. And no others were being born. We became infertile. Then we found Caesare, and it all changed. Within a short time of him living with us, ten women became pregnant. The number was unheard of. At first it seemed a coincidence and then we learnt that all of them had fed him at some time or other; by that I mean they had used their psychic energy to feed him the blood fruit.'

'Fertility is the most potent magic,' I murmured recalling one of Miranda's lessons.

I looked down into the nearest cot. The baby was a perfectly formed Allucian, no more than three or four inches long. It smiled at me. Its knowing eyes were both horrifying and beautiful. And something else: The irises were pulsing liquid gold in colour. Completely unlike the eyes of all the other Allucians I'd seen so far.

'How unusual,' I said.

'Yes. Unique.'

'So your babies have gold eyes?'

'Not usually.'

I turned to stare at Ilura and her face was grave for the first time since we had met. I glanced back at the infant and shuddered. It smiled back at me with a malevolence that I would never have considered possible.

'Is there anything else different about them?' I asked, watching the creature crawl around his cot.

'No, of course not,' she laughed. 'They are just babies.'

Then as if to prove her right the baby began to cry. As with all the Allucians it made no physical sound. Instead its face contorted as I watched. The nurse beside its cot responded immediately as though something had freed her from her catatonic state. She embraced the child, lifting it from the cot and took it from the room.

'Feeding time,' Ilura confirmed.

We left the nursery dormitory and Ilura led me to a ward of pregnant women. There were twenty more with child and each of the women, I noticed, had gold flecks in their eyes.

'We're evolving,' Ilura explained. 'And the council feels it is a good thing. This wonderful change has occurred because of Lord Caesare.'

'Are you so certain this is good?'

'Of course. No race can survive without adapting to their new world.'

But I wasn't so sure that the change was so wonderful. I glanced back at the nursery door, felt the glint of golden pupils glaring into my shoulders. I shrugged. They were just babies and the door was now closed. So how could they possibly be watching me? My imagination was running away with me.

Outside once more, I stood looking up into the fake sky, breathing air that could not possibly be as clean and fresh as it seemed. I couldn't help but fear the changes I had seen in my brother. He was more evil, yet somehow controlled it. He could no longer tolerate the sun. The evolution was working in both directions. I for one did not wish to be forced into the dark by my continued contact with the Allucians.

'Ilura,' I said panic rising in my chest. 'Help me.'

Her small hand closed over my arm. She led me shuddering back to the carriage.

'You have nothing to fear. No harm will befall you in our world,' she said soothingly.

We left the city. I was relieved to be once more in the garden, away from the blank gold stare of those unique children. All the time I could hear a lullaby in my head that I'd heard somewhere before but couldn't place. No matter how much Ilura patted and soothed me, I shivered all the way back. It was as if the mountain had become my tomb and the cold was seeping deep into my bones.

Prisoner

'Ilura explained things,' I said to Caesare that evening as we ate.

'I see.'

'I saw the nursery.'

Caesare didn't answer. He carefully cut into his rare steak and began eating. I reached for my filled glass of wine.

'Caesare, this whole situation. This world. We don't belong here. You realise that, don't you?'

'I can't leave.'

'Can't?'

I stood. My appetite had diminished since I arrived, and yet we went through a process of eating and drinking. It was very civilised behaviour in a seemingly civilised world.

'You've changed,' I told him.

'Ah. So you can see that? You see, Luci, I am not all bad.'

I turned to him, my arms folded across my chest. Caesare had stopped eating and he smiled at me like a man in love, hoping desperately to be understood.

'This isn't you.' I raised my hand towards him in a half gesture. 'You've changed beyond recognition. The sun burns you now. How can that be a good thing?'

'I have lived underground for many years.'

'How many?'

Caesare frowned. 'I ... don't remember exactly.'

'How do they keep you here?'

I felt a shift in the walls. The eyes were watching again, though they had not been obviously present since my first evening.

188

'Tell me how you came to be here.'

Caesare sat back in his chair. Confusion brought colour to his cheeks. I waited. He looked several times as if he was going to speak, appearing to be on the verge of remembering.

'They've wiped your memory,' I stated after a few moments. 'You can't tell me because you don't know. It's witchcraft of sorts, some form of binding spell. It may manifest itself in the intolerance to sun and it ensures your continued presence here. You can't leave during the day because you'll burn up. And we never know when it really is daylight here, do we?'

Caesare stood calmly. 'I'm happy here, Luci. They took me in, gave me a home and made me a God. Why on earth would you think I'm a prisoner?'

'Then leave, go out of the mountain for an evening.'

'I have no need to. All my needs are met here.'

I stared at him. My eyes revealing that I believed him to be a liar, a coward. Under the calm exterior I saw a shallow echo of residual fear. Something had happened, and maybe he intentionally refused to recall his phobias. Somehow that gypsy instinct I'd developed while travelling with Miranda knew it. Caesare was as much a prisoner as I was, even though he denied it to himself.

'Of course,' I agreed verbally. 'All your needs are met, even companionship now.'

'And love too, perhaps, one day?' He looked at me shyly. My heart warmed a little to that innocent expression in his eyes. I could see the hope of love blooming there still. Maybe that would be his salvation.

'I may love you once again,' I said. 'But only ever as a sister loves her brother. Nothing more.'

'For now I will be satisfied with that.'

Resigned, I sat down at the table once more and began eating my steak, which was still at the perfect temperature. All our needs and wants were met as long as we did not attempt to leave. I wondered what would happen if we ever did. As though hearing my thoughts, Caesare shuddered and we ate in silence. We were too afraid to think.

As I walked down the now familiar passage to my room, the torches burst into flame before me as always, but I recalled the corridors in the nursery. I remembered once more the appearance of infinity. My mind's eye evoked the image of the doors. There had been hundreds, each one I assumed must lead to a room. The doors were crammed close to each other, and they lined either side of the corridor.

I shook my head. I must be imagining it. My memory, usually accurate, seemed to be playing tricks on me. But then it was this place and its people. I shuddered, recalling the new generation of Allucians. They would grow and take over this world one day. An icy cold fist gripped my heart at the thought of the babies becoming powerful. Would they be satisfied ruling an underground world?

I felt golden eyes observing me and turned to gaze back down the now darkened passage. I peered into the gloom, expecting to see something but it was empty. Feeling strangely uneasy I rushed ahead, throwing myself into my room. Only when the curtain fell down over the doorway did I feel calm and safe, as though my rooms were somehow protected from the psychic reach of the Allucians. Being able to seek shelter from my gaolers was, however, a bizarre notion, for they could go anywhere they wished. But the whole situation was insane. Why was I running from monsters when I was a monster in my own right?

Chapter 39 - Lucrezia's Story
The Darkness

Miranda warned me of the darkness.

'Everything is foretold,' she said. 'All that we plan comes to nothing if it is not in the cosmic design.'

'What are you saying?'

'The future is already played out – you just haven't been there yet. Think of time as a series of doors that need to be opened. The doors are on many levels, and the third one may be placed behind the first.'

'Time?' I laughed. 'Time moves forward. There's no other direction for it to go.'

Miranda looked at me with her usual patience, shrugged and shook her head. I indulged her.

'All right then. Time as doors. Go on.'

'There's an alternative future coming for you, and you need to be prepared to meet it.'

'Caesare?'

'He will be linked to it. But he is not the enemy.'

I was relaxed enough to smile. 'Oh yes, he is!'

'Light the fire,' she instructed.

I sat down, staring at the wood, twigs and dry leaves until a slight spark formed and the fire caught.

'Good, you're improving. But keep practicing always. One day your mind and those flames will save you.'

I knew it was useless to ask her what this meant. Miranda was always ambiguous and would rarely explain herself. I put it down to her Romany upbringing. I heard her noncommittal expositions

191

every time she read a fortune. Once I asked her why she never told them the clear vision when I knew that she could read the future as plainly as she could see herself in a looking glass.

'The future is set. If I tell them all, they will try and change it. But hints will keep them on the right path. Besides, no one really wants to know the truth about their future. Most of our visitors only want approval for their lives here and now. But remember the doors,' Miranda repeated. 'And step through them in the right order.'

'How do I know what the right order is?'

'Instinct.'

'What happens if I go through a wrong door, then?'

'The very idea!' Miranda hissed as she sucked in a gasp of air.

She grew quiet for a moment, looking deeply into the flames. I waited patiently as she summoned the information from the fire.

'The darkness,' she confirmed finally. 'And if that takes you, you'll never be free.'

I thought carefully before asking her my next question. Miranda would explain herself directly if asked the right question. I didn't want riddles.

'What is the darkness?'

Miranda looked at me over the leaping tongues of fire and as usual the flames seemed to dance in her green eyes. She stared ahead in that mysterious way she had of gazing into the future, her eyes squinted as though she were looking into the brightest sunlight.

'What you need to consider is how to avoid it.'

I sighed. Her ambiguity exasperated me.

'And?'

A golden-eyed Allucian baby crawled up to the fire and looked at Miranda. She stretched out her hand to pat his black shiny hair as if he were some harmless pet.

'You see?' She looked at me and smiled. Her pupils dilated to liquid gold, pulsing like the flames in the fire. 'The darkness is already here.'

The King

'Dreams always mean something,' Miranda had once told me. 'Never ignore their advice.'

I stepped from the comfort of my bed and pulled on my robe. My head and body felt heavy, and not just because of the intense dream I had just awoken from. A feeling of disorientation made me feel dizzy and confused. The mountain seemed to be rocking and swaying like a ship caught in a violent storm. I rested my hand against the wall and the world steadied again. Something in the atmosphere of the mountain made my stomach clench with fear. I tied my robe and walked to the curtain doorway where I stood, shivering. It felt late, but the unnatural light of the mountain meant that time was subjective. The time was whatever the Allucians wanted it to be.

I lifted the tapestry and gazed down the passageway. It was unnaturally dark and yet there were shadows flickering in a light somewhere ahead, as though the Allucians were blending into the walls again, but moving constantly. I ran bare foot along the corridor.

The torches unusually remained unlit. Even so, my night vision was perfect and I soon arrived at the door leading out into the garden. Here I paused again. The door remained closed when invariably it opened automatically for me as I approached. I pushed at the entrance: it didn't move. I felt a slight sense of panic and I pushed again, this time using all of my strength.

The rock screamed in protest. It was as though the door hadn't been moved in centuries. It scraped against the fake lawn, yanking up clumps of turf as it swung wide. I entered the garden.

The fake sun was full above me and the garden bloomed and grew as normal, but all was abnormally quiet. Unlike the usual peaceful silence, this was an absence of sound which felt so, so wrong. And yes, it felt like late morning. I tried to sense the workers, but their blood trail evaded me. It was as if the world of the Allucians was all part of some elaborate dream that I had believed to be reality. I had finally woken and could sense nothing living in this world except the foliage.

I ran to the riverside, looked for the boat, willed it to appear. But it did not. Instead the water was mirror still. Some dramatic flaw had occurred in this perfect world. The magic of the Allucians had stalled. Did this mean that my own powers would now return? I summoned a flame to my hand and a cold blue fire appeared immediately.

My own witchcraft had been stifled all the time I had been here; now, however, the embargo was lifted. All the words of power that Miranda had taught me now floated behind my eyes. I could finally remember them. Whatever magic had taken and controlled my memories was now gone. Warmth flooded my cheeks with the realisation that I could now blast my way through the rock if I so chose. I would be free. And I ran around the garden, dancing, happy. But then I stopped.

Caesare stood in the garden. He reached forward, plucked a flower from its stalk and watched it shrivel and die in his hands. No new bloom burst from the stalk. The garden was dying.

I went to him and placed a hand on his shoulder.

'I need to talk to you. Is there anywhere we can go and not be overheard?'

'Luci?'

His intense gaze met mine and he seemed at a loss as to how to answer for a moment. He was on the verge of explaining something to me. I could see a new fear in his eyes. And then Ilura appeared and stood before us both.

'What is it?' he asked.

'The babies,' she answered.

'What's happened?'

'They are missing,' Ilura replied, looking around her as though they might be close by.

Miranda's warning from my dream suddenly became clear to me. 'They opened some doors.'

Ilura studied me intently. 'How do you know that?'

'Is anyone hurt?' Caesare asked.

Ilura bowed her head and tears seeped from her eyes. 'All the nurses are dead, but it almost seems as though through natural means. As though they went to sleep and never awoke.'

'They no longer need them,' I murmured, but I was ignored.

'We need to see the King.' Caesare's eyes were grave as he placed his hand on Ilura's shoulder.

'No! Caesare! That's impossible.'

'What are you both talking about? Why can't we see your father, Ilura?' I asked. 'Surely he must be told what has happened?'

'The "king" is not my father,' Ilura said solemnly.

'Then who is he?'

'Not who, what is he ...' Caesare responded.

The mountain garden began to rot around us. The plants shrivelled and died. The river level dropped and dried up leaving nothing but a dusty channel. The pool, however, was still. I stared down at the immobile water. It was as though someone had thrown a pebble into the water and it froze as the ripples panned outwards. I was looking at ripples frozen in real time. I shook away the paralysis the phenomenon caused and looked up.

The landscape grew barren around us. I could see the city in the distance as the trees shrank. The marble and rock buildings shuddered as though they would fall apart and that dizzy seasick feeling I'd experienced earlier made me feel once more unsteady on my feet. Ilura gripped Caesare's leg in fear.

'What's happening?' she cried and this time the sound came from her open mouth and not just her mind. Her hand flew to her mouth in terror and I realised that the Allucians world was truly broken; even their telepathy no longer worked.

'Come,' Caesare said, and he took Ilura up in his arms like a baby and began to run with supernatural speed across the deteriorating land. I ran alongside him, knowing full well that the final mystery would be solved and I would discover who and what was behind the power of the Allucians.

Rock tumbled down around us. The mountain was reforming itself, eradicating the very essence of the Allucians from it. The ground shuddered beneath our feet as we ran. I believed at any moment it would just crack open and swallow us into the rock. Just ahead a landslide of boulders clattered down, blocking our way as they tumbled to the ground, knocking and clattering together. The rock sounded strangely hollow as it smashed into and crushed the remaining plants. I watched as years of lichen grew over the boulders in seconds. A barren tree extended out from between a crack in the boulders, and the other pieces of rock moulded together to form perfect waves of age-worn slate.

'This way!' Caesare called and I turned to see him running for an opening to his left.

I vaguely recognised it as the gateway to the Allucian citadel.

Ilura's telepathy worked intermittently. Her thoughts and screams of fear came sometimes from her head and sometimes from her mouth. She tried to stifle the physical sounds but her terror was an abyss that threatened to swallow her. The Allucians had never lived without their magic and it was as though a limb was being ripped from her body. It hurt. I sympathised because I too had felt powerless without my own skills.

A piece of blue rock tumbled down from above us. I threw myself against Caesare and we fell aside just in time. The sky was literally falling in, and as it hit the rotting grass both reverted back to their former state of thick, grey rock. Tiny hailstones of sharp blue stone rapidly rained down on us. One hit Caesare's temple, leaving a nasty gash that bled profusely for a few seconds before healing. Caesare sheltered Ilura from the hail. We staggered on to the archway, zigzagging to avoid being crushed as larger lumps of sky-stone fell. Through the archway and we were at the citadel; the Allucian world was swiftly shrinking.

Magic was being sucked from the air. An Allucian male ran frantically from his home in front of us as the mountain swallowed the structure before our eyes, absorbing it and replacing it with a blank rock face.

'Oh my God!' I yelled, seeing the half-absorbed body of another male Allucian as he was digested by the mountain. Only half of his face and a few fingers protruded when the rock stopped moving. 'What is happening here? Was everything an elaborate illusion?'

'Time is restructuring,' Ilura cried. 'We carved our life from the darkness and now it's taking it back.'

'What did you people do?' I cried. But neither Caesare or Ilura answered me.

We continued to hurry forward. Around us the mountain closed in, and behind us the city fell and crumbled, becoming solid rock once more. The once-smooth streets became uneven slate, sharp spikes jutting out from floor and ceiling. Screams of the dying echoed around the cave. It was the most sickening torture chamber. The Allucians were being punished for their excesses; they were being digested by the very mountain that gave them shelter.

The illusion of daylight had now completely disappeared. We halted in what appeared to be a cavern. Stalactites and stalagmites extended from the hollow floor and ceiling as though the mountain itself was growing fangs.

Ahead of us stood the nursery, and as far as I could tell, its structure was holding fast.

'How can that be?' I asked. 'Why is the nursery still safe?'

'That's where he is kept?' Caesare gasped.

'Inside,' Ilura replied. 'Where else do you keep a king, but in a palace.'

'Or an asylum ...' I murmured but neither of them responded.

We entered the nursery building, but this time I was even more alert to the malevolent presence within. There was a strong sense of madness and evil in the air. I'd sensed it before, but now it intensified. Glancing back from the huge hallway to the entrance doors I watched the mountain world as the rock closed in against the building and stopped one foot from the door. The mountain creaked and shuddered as though it had met with a force more powerful than itself.

I fell to my knees. My own magic had been quelled and now I remembered all my spells; realised I'd forgotten them without knowing. Such had been the magic of the Allucians. But now the block was gone and my head was free again. Anger surged up into my mind and heart. I had been psychically drugged and made into a pliable vegetable. With the return of all of my faculties I could feel the malice in the air. Caesare and any remaining Allucians would now suffer the consequences for their crimes. And maybe I would be destroyed along with them.

Caesare placed Ilura down in the open hallway and she fell against him, sobbing loudly. It was a human sound, one I had never thought to hear in this world of silence. But my heart was cold to her.

'They are dead. All dead. My people, my family.'

'You brought this on yourselves,' I answered calmly.

Ilura cried harder, hysteria making her screams bounce around the hallway. But my brother had no sympathy for her now.

'Stop it!' Caesare said harshly. 'Show me what you've done.'

She fell silent at his words and looked up at him in terror. It was ironic. She and her people had been our gaolers and now she was terrified of Caesare's anger. My brother had grown in strength also over the course of leaving the garden. His abilities, like mine, had been stifled and subdued to make him controllable. Now I saw the anger and fury burning in his blood-coloured eyes. He pushed Ilura from him and she fell to the floor crying quietly.

Something echoed above us; a tiny sound, like the patter of small feet on a marble floor. I looked up the staircase that led to the nursery but didn't want to go there and investigate. Upstairs I could hear the cries of the remaining women; their labour had begun and twenty more babies would soon be born. Their malevolent presence would wreck havoc on the remainder of this world, I was sure. But that didn't scare me; what did was the thought of being sucked into the rock while still conscious, and I shuddered at the thought of the Allucian man I'd seen this happen to. Maybe he was still alive in there. It was too horrible a thought, even for a monster like me. But I stood up, tall and strong, remembering again my own strength. I could blast a hole into the rock with one word of power. The mountain would not hold me again.

Ilura continued to cry. I looked down at her coldly and then at Caesare. His anger was quieting. A woman screamed above us and Caesare looked up. I knew he was feeling apprehensive, perhaps even a little afraid now. The Allucians had imprisoned him for years, yet now that freedom seemed imminent he looked confused and uncertain. Then a change occurred. The scarlet colour seeped from his eyes and Caesare staggered back against the door frame. Within moments he gathered his composure and I knew that all his memories had returned.

'Where is he, damn it?' Caesare demanded, grabbing Ilura and dragging her to her feet. 'Show me!'

She screamed again in terror and fright.

'This way,' I said.

I heard music; a lullaby, faint and enchanting. We left Ilura still cringing on the floor and walked towards a set of double doors to the left of the stairs. Caesare pushed the doors open with a crash and walked forward. We could now feel the call of this obscure song as we entered a wide passage with doors leading off it on both sides.

'I saw this corridor when she brought me here yesterday. The double doors were open then.'

'What is it?'

'The doors of time,' I muttered.

'What do you mean?'

'Miranda told me. The wrong door will lead to the darkness.'

'Who is Miranda?'

I couldn't answer but took his hand and pulled Caesare forward. He clasped my fingers firmly and I felt for a moment transported to an innocent time where a brother and sister could hold hands; a time before our sin. His fingers trembled. Caesare no longer seemed like the cruel, vicious and bitter monster he had become, but a frightened child. Just like me.

The doors had a different essence to them. A strange and violent tumult rocked and pulled at their handles and knobs. A thousand screaming voices could be heard behind one. It was made of polished silver and I caught my reflection in it. I remembered seeing the same reflection in Joanna's hairbrush several lifetimes ago. *Déjà vu*. I shied away to the other side of the corridor as we passed the door. It sounded like the hell of our Christian world and I had no urge to visit it, even if some part of me felt I belonged there. Door after door, all different. One was plain white, silent. I put my hand on the frame and the cold-looking wood was red hot and burnt the skin from my fingers.

'Ouch!' I stared down at my healing skin, watched the blisters shrink and dissolve.

Caesare stroked the handle of another door. This one was made from a million different cuttings of hair, all brunette and all belonging to different people. The door bowed as he touched it and blood seeped through its keyhole. Caesare pulled his hand back sharply.

'What's happening?' he cried.

I shook my head, unable to reply, though the answer was on the tip of my mind, somewhere in my conversations with Miranda.

Further down the corridor I saw a door which inexplicably felt right to me. How would I know which one was right? I feared the darkness because Miranda had warned me of it, even though I didn't understand what it was.

'This one,' Caesare murmured.

He stopped by a door of knotted, whorled wood. It looked like old and rotten driftwood polished smooth by the actions of the sea.

'He's behind there.'

'The King?' I asked, but Caesare didn't reply.

'Where are the babies?' Ilura said, and I turned to find her behind us. 'They must be here too. They did this.'

Caesare shook his head. 'They are just babies. It's him. He's loose.'

Caesare stepped forward but I gripped his hand, holding onto him firmly. 'I need some explanations before I go in there.'

'We don't have time. But you're right, you shouldn't come through here. Wait with Ilura.'

'No,' I pulled at his hand, tried to hold him back.

Caesare looked at me for a moment. His eyes were watery.

'I'm sorry,' he said. 'I always loved you.'

Then he shook his hand free from mine and stepped forward, his fingers closing around the doorknob. Ilura ran before him and placed herself in his path.

'Please,' she begged. 'Don't let him out. You don't know what he's capable of.'

'I only want to talk to him.'

Ilura shook her head. 'You came here to find him. We knew that. Even though you swore allegiance, we knew all along that in your heart you wished to absorb his power. Caesare, being near his essence all these years has changed you and us. What do you think will happen when you see him in the flesh? Touch him?'

Caesare paused for just a second before viciously batting Ilura out of the way. She smashed back onto the marble floor. Her head cracked loudly and there was the sickening crunch of bone on bone.He opened the door.

Light, not dark, flooded the corridor and the strength was drained from my limbs as I narrowed my eyes to try and see into the blinding glow.

Then the door slammed closed behind Caesare and my brother was taken from view.

Ilura was in my arms. Blood seeped from her temple and her nose and I lay her broken body down on the floor to examine her wounds further. Her breathing was shallow and there was a strange and sickening looseness about her neck. Some remembered healing made me straighten her body and I tried to keep it in line with her neck as she opened her eyes and looked at me.

'What's in there?' I asked.

'The ultimate God,' she answered. Her lips moved and her voice was croaky. Blood flecked the corners of her mouth as she spoke.

'Ilura, I can't help unless I know more. Is he dangerous? Will he destroy my brother?'

'It's all a curse. He was cursed.'

'He once told me he sold his soul,' I answered, remembering the night Caesare tied me to his pentagram.

'It was disguised as a blessing, but she hates all men ...'

'Who?'

There was no answer. Ilura's eyes were frozen wide, her mouth slack.

I stood and looked at the door. The call was gone now, but I could hear nothing from inside. This corridor, this whole world, was not my world and I had been taken into the darkness unwilling. Therefore my doorway to my own future had to be here also. This was not my fight or my choice.

'Choose a door,' Miranda whispered. 'But choose right.'

I remembered her warning. That one day Caesare would attain

great power and would try to force me from my future. I had to block his return.

'Use the word,' she said. 'It means nothing to some, but has great significance to you.'

I drew my triskele symbol large in the air, covering the doorway, and I saw the faint blue of the symbols aura as it sunk into and barred the door. Then I said the word. My power word. It's a different one for everyone. But mine held the full force of my will as I demanded my life back.

'Isabella!'

As my last child's name crossed my lips, hard mountain rock grew over the entrance, sealing it forever. My brother was trapped and so was the King with him.

I turned and saw them then; ten pairs of eyes staring down the corridor. The malevolence was gone from the gold pupils but the babies were still an extraordinary sight. Some were standing, some were crawling. Miniature monsters. I knew that they held unfathomable power. But I had my strength back and I would fight them to the death if necessary.

'Find your own doorway, but never come into my world,' I warned and they shuffled back. They had seen enough.

I headed for the door I had seen earlier, knowing with a certainty that this was mine. It was of fine polished mahogany with golden cherubs engraved around the frame. Each of them bore the face of my children. There was no door handle, only a child-faced door knocker. I reached forward, caressing Isabella's image before rapidly knocking three times on the door.

I glanced back down the corridor. The babies were gone and the world of the Allucians was finally silent. The door swung open before me and candlelight poured into the corridor. Inside I could see my Parisian hotel room. With two steps I was back once more among my possessions and in my own world. I also knew that I had arrived back only seconds after Caesare had stolen me from my bed.

The mahogany door silently closed behind me and faded away

to become nothing more than a blank wall. I examined it for cracks but there was no trace. The door and the corridor were gone. I looked over at my bed and saw the covers and sheets hanging over the side. I straightened it up and lay on top. My 'normal' world would never know that I had been torn from my rightful path, and yet I had months of memories spent with the Allucians. Being back in my own time saved me from the darkness that Miranda spoke of.

Entity

'And so, the King seemed a distant memory and all of it perhaps an insane and vivid dream?' I ask.

Lucrezia nods. 'I put aside the memories of my brother and that world. Until now.'

Lilly and I stare at Lucrezia as she makes this final revelation. Is this the part of her story we need?

'A king?' Lilly shudders. 'Powerful? Evil?'

Lilly looks over at me.

'I don't know if he is evil, but certainly very powerful. His contact with the Allucians changed them and my brother. I suspect that they used him to source their supremacy. It was evil and wrong of them, even if they believed they had no choice in order to survive.'

'Did you feel drained as you stood outside the door?' I ask.

Lucrezia is thoughtful. She tips her head to one side and her eyes become vacant, as if she is looking back in time to study the corridor and the door once more.

'No, Gabi. But then there was some kind of ward on the door already. I suspect that it was crumbling though, and that this being was controlling the babies, making them alter the reality of their world in order to aid his escape.'

I stay silent. How do I broach the subject of our strange stalker?

'How long could your ward hold?' Lilly asks.

'I don't know. Indefinitely perhaps. It would take an incredible power to free them from the rock if nothing else. But that is the power the Allucians had and then lost. I've thought long and hard on the subject. Caesare has never returned for me, nor have I sensed his presence since that night. I assume that if he does, then the King will be free. But then, this king may well have destroyed my brother.'

'I suppose you have explored all the options. It is possible they were using the King to gain power,' I agree.

Lucrezia nods. 'Yes. But if he is so powerful, then how did they imprison him initially? Caesare seemed to have those answers, but didn't want to tell me anything. Maybe they did some kind of deal with the King until they learnt how to manipulate his strength. The Allucians were nothing once their magic was crushed, and their power had clearly been suppressing mine.'

I thought for a moment. On the surface, the Allucians had appeared to be benign. But how would the search for ultimate power affect any race? Maybe the Allucian Chief had believed his aim was ultimately good. They had, after all, stopped Caesare from hurting Lucrezia. But there were too many unanswered questions.

'So you're a witch as well?' says Lilly, changing the subject. "That's so cool.'

'I could definitely teach you some stuff,' Lucrezia says. 'I think perhaps you both should learn some spells. You never know when you'll need the.'

I look at Lilly and I see the fear I feel, reflected in her eyes. 'This king ...'

'Yes?'

'You're sure he was trapped?'

Lucrezia bites her lip in thought. 'I'm only certain that Caesare passed through a doorway and that something else was there. Ilura said it was the King, but I really don't know. Why are you so concerned about him?'

I tell her about the mysterious entity that passed over Lilly and me in Turin, and something of the events of the last few weeks.

'We felt nausea and intense weakness. I even felt like my lungs couldn't get enough air,' Lilly explains.

'And stomach cramps, you say?' Lucrezia looks unnerved as

we both nod. She stands, wrapping her arms around herself in a subconscious defensive stance. 'This thing you mentioned. I came across it too. About ten years ago.'

'Where?' I ask.

'Stockholm. But nothing since. I'd forgotten about it until now, but it was terrifying at the time. I had no energy at all, and suffered intense vertigo and sickness.'

'Yes. And we're not used to feeling weak,' Lilly says.

'It was clearly taunting us,' I say. 'And let's be honest, we were being followed.'

I glance around the coffee bar and my head begins to feel woozy. It is almost like being drugged. 'Gabi? You ok?' Lilly asks.

I shake my head, trying to clear it. My limbs feel weak, a dull pain begins to throb behind my eyes and pins and needles dance over the tips of my fingers as I reach for my coffee cup. Lilly is looking at me intently as though my sudden strangeness is apparent.

'Sorry. I'm fine. Really,' I say, but I'm not convinced.

Lilly strokes my leg under the table. I feel that familiar tingle of passion surge through my skin and feel better briefly. Her touch steadies me.

'Well, I'm not,' gasps Luci abruptly as she slumps in her chair. 'Something's wrong.'

Luci stretches out a hand to steady herself, and Lilly grabs her fingers. She looks up into Lilly's eyes, shocked by the instant relief she feels from the symptoms. But we don't have time to ponder this strange revelation as a sudden scream pierces the air.

There is a commotion outside. I stand on impulse, my strength fully returned, and run to the exit. Lilly and Lucrezia follow. The café leads into the department store where we rush through the crowd of post-Christmas bargain hunters and headlong down the escalator. At the main door we emerge onto Deansgate. It is a familiar place for me, having spent many months in Manchester. I glance up briefly at the apartment block next door. I still own the penthouse but it's rented out now through a local agent. Then I look down the street to the Marks and Spencer's store and the strangely incongrous ferris wheel.

I feel that strange confusion again. My mental faculties are working below par and I can't understand why. Lilly grabs my arm. Her nails bite into my skin and I notice she is also holding onto Luci. I look frantically down the street. There are screams and yells coming from all around and the bizarre sounds echo in the busy street. *Only we seem to notice.* A door slams shut, yet the sound doesn't make sense so I dismiss it. Then we see him.

He is feeding on a pregnant woman. Her back is bent over his arm as he rips out her throat. Blood bursts from her jugular and a small, stifled sound bubbles from her shocked lips. He eats sloppily, spilling blood down his victim. It splashes his black clothing and bloodies his chin. We watch him silently. I clench my fists in anger. This is too low, even for one of our kind. Still he guzzles on, ripping and tearing at the flesh of her now tattered throat.

It seems an age before the fiend becomes aware of us, and drops the woman carelessly to the floor. She makes no sound, dead before her skull connects with the pavement.

'Mother ...' the creature says simply, holding out his hand towards Lilly's face. 'You are so young, so beautiful.'

His fingers drip with the same thick black goo we saw covering his victims. His body seems to produce it. His hands are gnarled, his back distorted like a parody of Victor Hugo's fabled *Hunchback of Notre Dame.*

'Don't touch me,' Lilly says and his hand stops inches before her cheek.

He is dressed in black velvet, renaissance in style; yet covering his breeches and frock shirt, he wears a modern long-length leather jacket. His blond hair is swept back into a ponytail held in place by a leather thong. He is the archetypal vampire. Except for his hideous demeanour.

He is monstrous in every way, from his twisted and mutilated face to his normal hair. I wonder if this is our king and if so – is this our future? Perhaps all we are will become distorted. Maybe we will become our own portrait and, like Dorian Gray, our sins will show on our faces until we become too grotesque to be seen.

'Caesare!' Lucrezia gasps.

'No!' I cry. I have no idea how she can recognise her brother in this creature.

Caesare turns towards her. For the first time I see his eyes staring back at us. They are molten lava; a combination of red and gold swirls occasionally shot through with black. He looks like the devil himself. I fight the urge to shrink away from him as Lucrezia shudders and leans in closer to me, clearly terrified by the sight of him.

Obscenely the street continues to thrive as before. People pass over and through the body of the dead woman and they are unaware of this deformed monster before them. It is as though we are in another dimension, and yet still part of the present one.

'Lilly,' I whisper.

Lilly stands firm and I edge forward, reaching for her in an attempt to pull her farther away from him. Caesare's feral leer returns to her. His expression is adoring and completely insane.

'You love him. Is there no room in your heart to love us all, Mother?

'I'm not your mother; you have mistaken me for someone else,' she tells him calmly.

Caesare is confused. His hands fly to his face, fingers run through his hair pulling it free of its binding. He tears at his scalp like a madman.

'Why are you lying?' he screams.

Lucrezia walks forward, steeling herself against the onslaught. 'Brother, calm yourself. We are a family of sorts. But Lilly is the youngest of us, more likely your granddaughter. She couldn't possibly be your mother.'

Caesare looks up uncomprehending at Lucrezia. She flinches

at the insanity in his face. His fangs are exposed and he is foaming at the mouth like a rabid fox. He reaches for his sister but she falls back against me. I push her into Lilly as I rush forward, throwing myself in his way. The fight must be between two equals and I am certainly the strongest of the three of us. I fall on him, pushing him down onto the floor. My arm rams under his chin to prevent those thrashing fangs from tearing into me. He struggles beneath me, kicking and bucking in an attempt to throw me off. We roll into the road. A bus hurtles down the street and I brace as I expect it to hit us, but instead I feel the rush of wind, and a twisting nausea churns my insides. Confused, I watch the bus continue down the road, and now I know, we are not really here. But where indeed are we?

Caesare snaps his jaw, gnashing his bottom lip to a pulp in frustration and then he focuses his terrible gaze on my eyes and the energy is rapidly sucked from my body.

'No!' Lucrezia cries. 'Stop it, Caesare! Please ...'

I feel my life slipping away as blackness squeezes my chest, emptying my lungs of air. He throws my weakened body off him, then stands and shouts in rage and lunacy at the passing crowd. But they cannot see his horrible, deformed face, twisted in pain and anger. The traffic and the people move steadily by. Some stop to browse in shop windows, helplessly unaware this crazed monster stands so near, ready to steal life from them. Caesare grabs a passing businessman and throws him into the road as a car drives full pelt through a red light. I watch through my blood-filled gaze as his body hits the front fender and is thrown several feet into the air. I turn away, staggering to my feet and I hear the body reacting to gravity as it smacks down onto the road. A dull crack echoes through the air as his back is broken in two places.

Caesare reaches for a woman but Lucrezia and Lilly are holding him back, though neither touches him. Lilly's commands keep him at bay, but he is a snarling, feral animal and seems incapable of rational thought.

'You're slowly being swallowed by the darkness,' Lucrezia tells him, her hands held up in a placating gesture and I wonder if she has dealt with the insane in her long medical career. 'Caesare! You have stayed away from your natural time path too long.'

But the monster doesn't understand.

'Listen to her,' Lilly says. 'Perhaps we can help you.'

'Mother. I brought you gifts,' Caesare gurgles through his teeth and blood. 'Why didn't you take my offerings?' His roar is one of the deepest agony and pain.

So, he was never trying to goad us. His reference to bringing us gifts reminds me of the behaviour of cats, who often bring their owners mice and birds to show their appreciation of the food and home they had been given. With his slack jaw, fierce teeth and lunatic expression, Caesare is the most unlikely pet I have ever seen.

Lucrezia crushes her hand to her mouth, tears welling in her eyes as she gazes at the brother she briefly loved. He has outwardly become the vile creature he was always inside. The darkness is eating him away. I can see the decay through my hazy vision.

'I thank you for the gifts,' Lilly tells him, clearly playing along. 'But now you must stop this. This is not our way, Caesare. You have exposed us all to the world with your reckless behaviour.'

I recognise the authority of a mother in her reasonable voice. Caesare falls to his knees in remorse.

'I never meant ... I only wanted ... I need your love, Mother, to make me better.'

'No, brother,' Lucrezia says. 'You need the light. It's the only way that darkness can be truly banished.'

With tears in her eyes she approaches the prone figure. He raises his humped form and stares at her, his eyes crazed and rolling.

'I love you,' she tells him. Then, in one fluid movement, she punches her hand hard at his chest, thrusting right inside through the rotting skin and bone and grasping his heart in her hand. She pauses, looking into his eyes for a moment, before pulling it out of his body. For a moment we watch it beat in her small hand. Caesare stares at his vital organ in shock. She says her word of power, only this time it is the name of her first child.

'Antonio.'

The heart bursts into blue flames. At the same time a sapphire inferno ignites inside Caesare's chest. He falls back, beating at the flames. But his swatting does no good, as cold blue flame rapidly eats him from the inside out. His body thrashes wildly, feet and arms smashing down on the concrete slabs, cracking the stones, black ichor dripping over the pavement. His body melts. The face, hideous though it was already, disintegrates into a black oily pulp and his entire body collapses in on itself, leaking onto the road in a growing puddle of darkness. Caesare is now nothing more than a hideous stain on the street.

Lucrezia still stands, hand outstretched, holding his heart. As we watch, the organ turns to powder in her hand, slowly slipping away like the sands of time through her pale fingers, to scatter in the wind. As the last of his presence dissolves, breaking down further into black dust, I feel the power returning fully to my limbs. I stumble forward, taking the sobbing Lucrezia into my arms and stretching out a hand to my darling Lilly. We stagger away from the scene of the crime. Our enemy is dead but it still feels like we have more questions than answers. As we reach the doorway to the department store once again, I glance back at the street and see the body of the pregnant woman fading away from this reality. It will end up in another place, hiding the crime, but I have no idea where that will be.

Epilogue
Present

We return to the café. Our drinks are where we left them. We sit down and look at each other in silence as though we never left the table in the first place.

'It's over,' says Lilly.

Lucrezia and I, however, are still uneasy. Something is still wrong and we can both feel it.

A sense of unreality slowly seeps into my shocked brain as I look around the cafe. I feel as though I am out of step with time. It is like I am a visitor in my own dimension.

The sound in the coffee bar decreases. Until now, the distant chatter of an old couple on the table near us has steadied and levelled the normality of the day. I look around. In the corner of the room a mother feeding her child in a highchair melts into the tacky Monet print behind her. They become painted pastel figures and part of the beach scene. The waitress walks through a wall that wasn't there moments before. A teenage girl is sucked into her coke glass, the glass into the table and finally the table into the floor. The room is fading around us. I reach for Lilly and Luci as I rise to my feet seconds before my chair melts into the flowery carpet. Around us the world has changed and the walls have faded to become the shadow of countless doors and the remaining furnishings fade into the rock that is suddenly established beneath our feet.

All three of us are standing looking down an immense corridor. Doors of all makes, all styles and eras, and made of different materials, line both sides.

Just as Lucrezia described in her story. This is the remains of the Allucian nursery.

I try to hold Lilly's hand but her body seems insubstantial and my fingers grasp only air.

'The corridor of time,' Lilly murmurs. 'I remember ...'

'What's happening?' I say.

Lucrezia looks at me and then stares down the corridor at ten pairs of shining gold irises. But the babies come no further towards us. They merely look benignly back as though waiting for us to choose our new pathway. I wonder if they are the keepers of the corridor now.

'That's the door,' Lucrezia points to the wall, but all I see is a rocky space between two other doors.

'How on earth did we get here?' I ask.

'Yes, the door,' Lilly says walking forward.

Lilly examines the rock and I can see and feel an immense power emanating from the wards. The triskele glows as though cut from blue light. Lucrezia is shivering as she stares at her handiwork.

'It seems secure,' she murmurs.

'Then how did he get out? And more importantly how did we get here?' I ask. For I know without a doubt that something else is about to happen.

'Have we travelled back in time?' Lilly asks.

'I don't think so.' Lucrezia turns and looks both ways. 'There's no pull to any door. This is clearly an illusion.'

Her tears have dried but her eyes are sad. I reach for her, find her as solid as myself. We both turn to see Lilly moving down the corridor with intent. I try to move after her, but I'm thrown back. My darling lover gets further away. I see her halt in front of a door. Her hand reaches out.

'No!' Lucrezia yells. 'Don't touch it!'

The door springs open as though it has a life of its own. Lilly face is ecstatic as she is drawn through. She looks like she is going home.

I drag myself forward, pulling hard against the force. As I reach Lilly she steps through the door and I fall at the foot of it. It's made of carved rock and ornate marble, like the doorways to temples and holy places portrayed in renaissance art.

'Lilly!' I cry.

The doorway is a howling gale. I cannot reach it. Lilly is on the other side and remains unaffected by the wind. She steps deeper in and now I can see a beautiful garden on the other side. I touch the frame of the door. It burns the skin from my fingers. I yelp in pain but my hand still flies out before me. But I am too late. The door slams shut. I see one fleeting glimpse of Lilly, looking up into the sky, an expression of happiness and wonder colouring her face as the sun bursts through the clouds and beams down on her like a holy light.

'Lilly!'

Lucrezia is holding me. We are back in the café. I open my eyes and look around. People are looking at us strangely and I realise I have had some form of hallucination.

'What happened?'

'We're back,' she says.

'I had this strange experience.'

'I know.'

I sit up and look for Lilly. Her seat is empty.

'No ...'

'I'm sorry,' Lucrezia says. 'I don't know what happened.'

'You did this! It's witchcraft!'

'No! I swear it wasn't me.' Lucrezia drops her head into her hands. 'At least, I don't think it was me.'

'Where is she?' I demand.

Lucrezia shakes her head. Her face is deathly pale and the strength and vitality she always possesses seems sucked from her.

'You have some explaining to do.'

'I think talking about the corridor summoned it. But I don't understand why. Lilly went through a door of her own free will,' Lucrezia explains.

'No, she seemed drawn.'

'Then she was meant to go through it.'

No. The last person we knew of to go through a door came back a hideous and twisted being. I couldn't bear to lose Lilly, but it would be so much worse if she returned insane and we had to destroy her. My head falls into my hands. Nausea pulls at my insides. I feel as though I am on the brink of finally losing my mind. After all the losses of the centuries, my son and daughter, every woman I had loved, none of them hit me as hard as this moment.

My mobile phone rings in my pocket. I feel the vibration, hear the musical tone of Sam Sparro, but don't respond. I'm in shock. I've lost the love of my life and have no way of knowing how to find her. She may be anywhere in time.

'Aren't you going to answer that?' the waitress asks as she clears our table.

I put my hand in my pocket; fumble around like a blind man and eventually I grip the phone, pulling it free and out into the restaurant. Around us the other customers dart furtive glances our way.

'For goodness sake,' mutters the old woman on the next table. 'Young people never know when to turn those things off.'

I glance down at the number that's calling. It's an international call and I don't recognise the number. My fingers are numb as I press the receive button and place the handset to my ear but find I am incapable of speech.

'Gabi! It's Lilly. I know this is really strange after so long, but I need you. I'm in Stockholm.'

I listen, not quite believing it's her.

'Darling! Lilly? How can that be? You've only just vanished!'

'What?'

'Just ten minutes ago... Darling, I'm so relieved to hear your voice.'

'Ah,' Lilly responds. 'I have so much to tell you.'

216